Gainer

Jagged Edge Series #6

A.L. Long

Interior edited by H. Elaine Roughton
Cover design by Laura Sanches

ISBN: 978-1546840565
This book is intended for mature audiences only

Acknowledgment

To my husband of many wonderful years, who is with me heart, body and soul through each word I write. If it weren't for him my dream of writing would have never been fulfilled. I love you, sweetheart. And to my family, whom I also love dearly. Through their love and support, I can continue my passion for writing.

To the many readers, who took a chance on me and purchased my books. I hope that I can continue to fill your hearts with the passion I have grown to love.

Most of all I want to thank my incredible PA, Barbara Danks. I don't know where I would be without her and to my wonderful Street Team (Athena Kelly, Lori Hammons, Kristen Ann Tanner, Marsha Black, Heather Swan, Sallie Ann). You ladies have been a godsend.

Gainer: Jagged Edge Series #6

Table of Contents

CHAPTER ONE

Gainer

Drinking the rest of my brew, I stood, making my way to the kitchen to deposit my empty bottle in the trash. When I returned, the guys were still sitting around discussing the bachelor party for Sly. The initial plan was to have it at Ash's place, but Sly and Nikki thought it would be better to elope to Las Vegas. Personally, it didn't matter to me either way. All of us at Jagged Edge were brothers and supported each other no matter what. There were nine of us in all. Peter Hewitt started Jagged Edge Security. When he asked us to be a part of his team, how could we say no? We were brothers. Ash Jacobs was our explosives expert, Cop Coppoletti worked with weapons, while Sly Capelli was more of a pain in the ass than anything, although he was great at sneaking up on people. Then there was Mike Chavez, who knew everything about mechanical things. If you had something that needed fixing, he was the guy. There were even Ryan and Josh Hyatt. Those two were actually brothers, but by the way they disagreed on things, you couldn't tell. We ended up losing Hawk Talbott as part of the team. No one could blame him, though. If I had a woman as beautiful as Isabelle, I would have moved anywhere to be with her. Even if it meant changing my lifestyle to become a diplomat and a prince. Who would have thought? We even managed to gain a woman on our team. Nikki Jennings, soon to be Nikki Capelli. She had proven to be a great asset. It was a place we all called home, and now instead of fighting on a battlefield, we all work together.

When I got home, the first thing I did was check to make sure I didn't have any messages on my answering machine. It was the same as every other day, nothing. I wasn't sure why I continued to torture myself. Ten years is a long time to wait for something that was never going to happen. As much as I wanted to believe that she would call, I was just fooling myself. I will never forget the day that she reached out to me, letting me know that she wanted to meet. My biological mother was what they called her. I was finally going to meet the woman who left me on the steps of St. Vincent's so many years ago, only that day never came.

En route to my room, I threw my jacket on the chair and began removing my clothes. Slipping under the covers, I stared at the ceiling, wondering what my life would have been like had she actually shown up. I wasn't sure why I kept thinking about her. Maybe it was because I hated her for doing what she did. Realizing what I just thought, I pushed from the bed and headed to the kitchen, where the answering machine was sitting on the counter. I disconnected the machine and tucked it away in the closet. The only reason I had that stupid machine was because of her. Heading back to bed, I was finally able to fall asleep.

~****~

"It's such a nice day, Louis, why don't you go outside with the rest of the boys? You need to learn how to interact with them instead of spending so much time by yourself."

"But I don't want to, Sister Claire. The boys are always making fun of me. I hate them. I hate this place."

"Fuck! This shit has to stop," I hissed in the silence. I'd had the same dream for more than eighteen years. Not even the shrink at the army base could help me get over the nightmares. Knowing there was no way that I was going to be able to go back to sleep, I pushed from the bed and headed to the bathroom to do my thing. Grabbing my cell from the end table, I saw it was only 5:00 a.m., which for me was way too early, especially since I left the shop not more than four hours ago.

Glaring at my reflection in the mirror, I knew I had to find a way to put this behind me once and for all. I just didn't know how, other than facing the problem head on. I knew that was never going to happen, at least not for now. In the meantime, I needed to do something to clear my mind. Slipping on my sweats and my shoes, I decided a couple of laps around Central Park Reservoir would help me do that.

The park was quiet as I made my way past the Balcony Bridge. I loved running in the park. It was the only way that I could really clear my head. When I first began working for Jagged Edge, one of the must-haves was finding a place that was close enough to the park to go running. So, when Peter found the two-bedroom condo apartment near the park, I couldn't pass it up. He even managed to find one with windows facing the park. What a guy.

After a great run and feeling the burn in my lungs, I decided to head back to my apartment and get cleaned up. I still had a few hours before I needed to be at the YMCA for my class. Being a martial arts instructor was another thing that I used to clear my mind. I began training in martial arts when I left the orphanage and joined the military. The base doctor thought that it would be a good way to help me control my anger issues. At least he was right about that. Helping out those kids, and giving them the self-confidence that was taken away from me, was the best thing that I could have done. For this reason, I dedicated an hour a day, three times a week to these kids.

As I was leaving the park, not paying attention where I was going, I plowed her completely over. The bag that she was carrying went flying in the air and her body landed on the hard surface, with her shoulder hitting the sidewalk first. I tried really hard to catch her before she fell, but I wasn't quick enough. Squatting down to her level, I took hold of her arm and asked with concern. "Are you okay? I am so sorry. I wasn't paying attention where I was going."

"Yeah, I think I'm okay," she replied in a soft, timid voice.

"Here, let me help you up." Holding my hand out to her, I waited for her to comply.

When she placed her hand in mine, I looked down to see that my larger hand had engulfed her smaller one. When she was on her feet, I looked her over to make sure she was okay, confirming what she had said. It was then that I noticed she had a scrape on her elbow that was caused by the fall. Taking hold of her arm, I tried to get a closer look, but she pulled her arm away from me. Placing my hands in the pockets of my hoodie, I mentioned, "You have a pretty good scrape on your elbow," as I watched her turn her arm so she could get a better look.

"It will be fine," she claimed. "It looks a lot worse than it is."

Grabbing her bag, which looked like it had been through hell, I handed it over to her. When she took hold of it and looked up at me, I saw she was actually very beautiful. Taking a better look at her, I realized that she was wearing a maid's uniform, which told me she must work at one of the hotels close by.

There was something about her eyes that told me she was about ready to collapse. Her small frame began to wobble back and forth, only this time, I caught her before she fell to the ground. Picking her up, I walked over to a park bench and carefully set her down. I waited for a few minutes until her focus came back.

"Are you sure you are okay?" I questioned concerned.

"Yeah, Just a little hungry. I got so busy at work that I didn't have time to eat," she confessed.

Considering her explanation, I looked at her again and realized that she did look thin for her build. To me, it looked as though she missed more than one meal. Doing the gentlemanly thing, I offered, "Can I take you to breakfast? It's the very least I can do since I ran you over."

"You really don't need to do that. I will be fine."

"But I want to. Come on. There's a small café about a block away."

There was no way that I could accept 'no' for an answer. Rising to my feet, I held out my hand and waited for her to take it. She hesitated for a moment, but then finally placed her hand in mine. When I offered to carry her bag for her, she gave me a disapproving glance and held on tightly to it. I wasn't sure why she wouldn't allow me to carry it for her. My guess was that she wasn't a very trusting person and probably thought that I was going to run off with it.

When we reached the small café, it was just getting ready to open, which was perfect. This café was one that I liked going to in the early morning, and the only one that opened at 6:00 a.m. As we stepped past the waitress that was holding the door open for us, she winked and said, "Sit wherever you'd like. Coffee will be done in a sec."

Smiling back at her, I looked over to the young woman at my side as I held up two fingers, letting the waitress know to bring two coffees. Choosing to sit at a booth away from the door, I slid in one side while my breakfast guest slid in the other. Picking up a menu, I asked, "Do you mind if I ask you what your name is?"

"Emma," she answered as she kept her head down, hidden behind the menu.

"I'm Lou. It's nice to meet you, Emma."

I held out my hand for some time before she finally shook it. While I was trying to figure her out, the waitress showed up with two coffees, cream, and sugar. Since I came here quite often, I already had an idea of what I was going to order, so before the waitress could ask, I said, "Three eggs, wheat toast, bacon, and a side of pancakes."

"How about you, Miss?" the waitress asked.

"I will have the same, but can you add hash browns and sausage?" she replied.

Wow! She must have been really hungry. I was pretty certain that there was no way she was ever going to be able to consume all of that food. Giving her an unbelieving look, she rolled her eyes and said matter-of-factly, "I'm starving, and since you invited me, I'm not holding back."

"Not a problem, Emma. Eat to your heart's content," I countered, content with her order.

CHAPTER TWO
Emma

After offering to help Courtney finish cleaning her last junior suite, I accidently bumped a black briefcase while trying to maneuver the vacuum around the king-sized bed. I wish that it had never popped open, but there it was, staring right at me. The case was filled with some documents along with money. Normally I wouldn't have looked twice, but it was like it was telling me to help myself, so I did. Checking to make sure that Courtney was still cleaning the bathroom, which I knew would take her at least fifteen minutes, if not more, I began picking up the bundles of cash and taking a few bills from each one. It might have been easier to take the whole bundle, but this wasn't my first rodeo. I didn't want to risk any suspicion that there was any money missing.

Hearing the toilet flush, I knew that Courtney was close to being finished. Stuffing the money wherever I could inside my bra and under my uniform, I continued dusting as though nothing had happened. Hearing her behind me, I asked with a smile, trying to hide my guilt, "Are we ready to blow this popsicle stand?"

"Yepper, "she replied, pulling her rubber gloves off her hands.

One thing about Courtney, no matter how shitty the day was, she always managed to make it seem better. Heading out of the room and down the hall to the service elevator, Courtney held the door while I pushed the supply cart into the elevator. I was thankful that this was the last room that needed to be cleaned for the day. I was starving and hadn't eaten a decent meal for two days. At least now, with the money I had taken, I would be able to stock up on my supply of Raman noodles and water. A new blanket would also be nice.

Reaching the employee lounge, I stuffed all of the cash I had just taken into my bag, closed my locker, and exited through the hotel doors, taking my normal route to the shelter, which was down Madison to Fifth Avenue and into Central Park. While I was repositioning my bag on my shoulder, I felt like I got hit by a train. No way was the guy who ran into me watching where he was going. He knocked me over, and the minute I used my arms to break the fall, the pain began to radiate through my elbow. Looking up to the guy, I forgot about the pain when my eyes met his. He was the most gorgeous man I had ever laid eyes on. When he held out his hand to assist me to my feet, I was afraid that he would burn me with his hotness.

My heart just about sank when he grabbed my bag. It wasn't that I thought anything would fall out of it, it was the fact that it was old with a zipper that really didn't work, I was afraid that the contents may have shifted, causing the money that I had tucked under my things to surface. It was only after he handed my bag to me that I felt better. Holding it close to my body, I was about to go on my way when he began talking to me. After a few shared words and his invitation for breakfast, I was walking with him to a small café. I was so hungry that it would have been stupid of me to decline his offer.

After I sat across from him, we placed our order. Sipping my coffee, I couldn't help but stare at this guy, whom I just found out was named Lou.

"So, based on your uniform, I'm guessing you work at one of the hotels," he offered as I continued to sip my coffee.

"Yeah. I work at the Park Lane Hotel," I replied.

"So, you enjoy that kind of work?" he asked.

"Not really, but when it is all that is out there, you can't nitpick about where your income comes from," I pointed out.

I couldn't have been happier when our order showed up. Keeping my mouth full of food and my head down, I avoided any other questioning on his part. All I wanted to do was finish my meal and get the hell out of there. Maybe even find a nice warm motel where I could stay for a night or two.

Finishing my last bite, I wiped my lips and began to place the shoulder strap of my bag over my arm. I wasn't even off of the seat when Lou asked, "Can I walk you to your place?"

My throat began to constrict as I tried to make up an excuse as to why he couldn't walk me. "I don't think that is a good idea," I began as I proceeded to scoot across the booth seat. "I don't know you very well and I really don't feel good about letting you know where I live. If you don't mind, I will just be on my way. Thanks for breakfast."

"Can I at least have your number?" he asked, pushing from the booth himself.

"No can do. I don't have one to give," I confessed, knowing that everyone had a cell. At least, everyone except me.

"How will I see you again?"

"Maybe we'll bump into each other again," I replied with a sarcastic smile.

As I opened the door, I could tell that Lou wasn't too happy with my frankness, but the last thing I needed was a handout. I had made it on my own for the past nine years and I didn't need any handouts now.

~****~

It always seemed like the same thing over and over. Standing outside the building with so many others needing a place to sleep, I just missed my chance to get in and was ultimately turned away. Even though it was still pretty early in the morning, I guess having breakfast with Lou wasn't such a good idea after all. I was hoping I would be able to hold on to the money I took for a little longer, but unless I wanted to sleep under the bridge again, I needed to spend some of it. Turning on my heels, I headed down the street to the nearest motel that looked to be clean and reasonably priced.

Finding just the right place, I checked in and paid my sixty bucks, I headed to my room for the night, which was located just up the stairs and to the right, just as the clerk instructed. As I opened the door, I could smell the scent of clean linens, which was a definite plus compared to what I was used to. Placing my bag on the bed, I began taking a look around the room. Even though the furniture looked like it came out of the seventies, the room was clean and nicely decorated. Stepping inside the bathroom, I was surprised to see that there were fresh towels hanging on the rack that were as white as the first snow. As I pulled back the shower curtain, the shower was also very clean. So clean that it was calling my name. Stripping off my maid's uniform, I found a missed hundred dollar bill stuck between the material of my uniform and skin. Kissing the bill for good luck, I placed it on the counter and finished getting undressed.

The water felt so good on my skin. I couldn't remember the last time I had taken a real shower. Pulling the curtain just enough to see the toilet, I grabbed the complimentary bottle of shampoo and conditioner that had I placed there, along with the plastic shaver. *"All the comforts of home,"* I thought to myself as I let out a small chuckle. I wasn't even sure what those comforts were.

Finished with my wonderful shower, I wrapped a towel around my damp body and another around my wet hair. Filling the sink full of soapy water, I began washing my uniform, making sure that it was clean for the next day. Swishing it in the warm water a few times, I drained the sink and wrung out the excess water before draping it over the shower bar to dry. One thing nice about staying in a motel was that I would be able to iron out the wrinkles once the uniform was dry.

Settling on the bed, I just stared at my bag, unable to bring myself to open it. Pulling it closer with shaky hands, I slid the zipper back slowly, revealing the money that was lying on top. There was so much of it. Taking a deep breath, I emptied the contents of my bag onto the bed and began counting the money.

By the time I had finished, there was exactly $14,940.00, and that included the hundred-dollar bill still in the bathroom and the one I broke to pay for this room. It was the most money I had ever held in my hands. Thinking that I may have gone a little overboard with what I took, I promised myself that I would be returning all but a few thousand dollars in the morning when I got to work. I just needed to figure how I was going to do that.

Putting the money in a couple of envelopes that the motel had left for guests to use in case they wanted to write a letter, I placed the money back in my bag along with the rest of my things, while leaving a change of clothes out to sleep in. Changing into a long t-shirt that had seen better days and a pair of plain white panties, I turned down the covers and got beneath them, pulling my bag to my side with my hand wrapped around the handle. This was a daily ritual with me. When you didn't have much, you tended to protect what you did have. Finding the remote, I began going through the channels until I found something that I wanted to watch. It must not have been too exciting, because my eyes began to get heavy and soon I was sleeping.

~****~

At first, I thought that I might have been dreaming. Checking under the covers to make sure that my bag was still secured around my wrist, I flipped off the covers and headed to the door. The person on the other side was still knocking when I got to the door. Opening it until the chain I secured prevented it from opening further, I could see that it was the guy from the front desk who checked me in. Peeking my head through the crack, I asked in a husky voice, "Is there a problem?"

"No, Ma'am. Just thought you might want to know that there is a vending machine on the main floor and an ice machine as well. I forgot to let you know when you checked in," he confessed.

"Well, thank you for the information," I replied.

When the guy left, I thought it was strange that he didn't just call my room and let me know. It would have been the easiest thing to do. Closing the door, I decided to take the guy up on his offer. I hadn't eaten since this morning and it would be nice to go to work with a little something in my stomach. Slipping on a pair of jeans, I pulled a few small bills from the envelope and headed down the stairs to the vending machine.

When I closed the door, I could hear sirens going off in the distance. Looking over the balcony in the direction they were coming from, I realized that I could see the Park Lane Hotel. As I looked over to the hotel, I realized it was there that the sound of sirens was coming from. Just as the police arrived, the paramedics and the fire department also arrived. As I kept my eyes fixed on the commotion, it was way better than watching any movie on TV. Even though a large crowd began to form, I was up high enough to see that the paramedics were hauling what I presumed was a dead body on the stretcher, based on the black body bag lying on the top. That kind of excitement never happened while I was working.

After watching for about an hour, the crowd finally settled and began to break up. With nothing else to see, I headed down the stairs to grab a snack from the vending machine. Tomorrow when I got to work, I would need to find out from Courtney what happened. She knew everything that went on in the hotel, sometimes even before it happened. It was kind of scary the way she could do that.

CHAPTER THREE
Gainer

What a strange, but beautiful girl. She was definitely one of a kind. I really didn't spend enough time to get to know her, but at least I knew what she did and where she worked. Watching her leave the little café, I looked to see which direction she was headed until she was out of sight. Placing a few bills on the table to cover the tab, I headed out towards the park, to my place.

Given the hour of the morning, Central Park was beginning to come to life with people either getting a dose of their daily exercise or just to enjoy the wonderful weather. Me, all I wanted to do was get to my place and take a shower, then head to the shop to see what the guys were up to. Taking it easy, I began jogging at a slow pace through the park. Just as I headed over the Gapstow Bridge, I noticed an older man, in his fifties, chatting with a young boy who appeared to be lost. The minute the man turned towards me, my gut began to churn. *"What the hell? No, it can't be."* I began thinking to myself as I got closer to the man. Even though it had been over eighteen years ago, I would know that face anywhere.

Walking up to them, I took hold of the man's arm and hissed, "Stay away from him."

The man, whom I knew to be Father O'Malley, looked at me like I was out of my mind. Pulling his arm from my grasp, he cursed, "Do you mind telling me what is going on, young man?"

Before I could say another word to the man I hated more than I hated anyone in my life, the little boy's mom walked up to us. "Oh, my God, Joey, are you okay? I told you to stay near," she said hysterically as she took the little boy in her arms. Looking over to Father O'Malley, she stood and praised him. "You are a godsend, Father. Thank you so much for keeping him safe."

Right then, I just about lost it. He was no more a godsend than I was the Pope. Pulling my gaze away, I looked to the woman and warned, "If I were you, ma'am, I wouldn't trust this man again. Your son was lucky this time."

"Don't be silly. He is a man of the cloth," she replied as she held her son by the hand and began walking away.

As I reverted my gaze back to the pedophile, he was gone. Glancing up the path, I couldn't see him. I knew he couldn't have gotten far. Jogging down the trail, I began searching for him. I wasn't done telling him what I thought about him. Concerned about finding him, I began to wonder what he was doing in Manhattan. He was a priest at St. Vincent's in Chicago. He shouldn't be here. Knowing that he slipped away from me, I cut across the park and headed to my apartment.

What seemed like a great start to a beautiful day just turned into a day I wanted to remove from my calendar. Never had I left my apartment building without my keys. As soon as I felt inside my pocket, I knew I had done just that. Pushing every button on the entrance pad, I stood outside and waited for someone to let me in or answer my call. Not long after I finished pressing the last button, the door buzzed open. I wasn't sure who it was that let me in, but thank God.

~****~

Walking into the shop, I could see that Peter was busy at his computer doing his normal daily thing. Peeking my head inside, I said a quick "Hello" before heading to the conference room. Before I could leave, Peter said, "Hold on, bro."

Taking a seat in front of his desk, I waited until he was finished with what he was doing. His fingers were going a mile a minute on the keyboard. When he was finished, he looked up to me and shared, "I guess there was a situation at the Park Lane Hotel. They have requested additional security. Seems someone was murdered in one of their Junior Suites. We should be receiving information soon on who it was."

"Wait, did you just say the Park Lane Hotel? I accidently ran into a maid that works there early this morning," I admitted.

"Well, that could be a good thing. Maybe she could give us some insight on what happened," Peter replied.

"I don't know if that is even possible. I don't know if I will ever see her again. And besides, I get the feeling that she likes keeping to herself."

"No matter, either way, we will find out what happened to that guy."

After, I left Peter's office, I began thinking about my encounter this morning and the funny way Emma acted. I knew that Manhattan was a big city and a girl needed to be careful, but the way she acted was more like a person hiding something, especially the way she held onto her bag and disappeared so quickly after our meal.

Booting up the computer, the minute it came to life, I wanted to find out why in the hell Father O'Malley would be in Manhattan or if there was any other information on him. Seeing him was like seeing a ghost from my past, and it was something that I needed to put to rest once and for all. Typing his name in the search engine, a whole bunch of nothing showed up except for one link that seemed to pop out. Seems Father O'Malley was in Manhattan to attend the ordainment of a new priest to St. Peter's. This would explain what he was doing here. It still didn't sit well with me knowing that he was here, but at least I knew where he would be. It was time that I faced my demons and had a little chat with him.

As I was shutting down the computer, Sly entered the room looking like he was just run over by a truck. Looking his way, I said, "Dude, you look like shit."

"Thanks a lot, Gainer. Guess I should have left before Cop pulled out the Crown," he confessed.

"Glad I wasn't here to witness that."

"Yeah, I'm gonna grab some java. Maybe that will bring me to life."

Smiling at Sly, I patted him on the back and said, "Good luck with that. Catch you later."

Crazy Sly. I could only imagine what it was going to be like in Vegas once he and Nikki got married. Letting Peter know that I was leaving, I got in my Tundra and headed down the road to St. Peter's. Basically, being raised in a Catholic church, I knew that their doors were always open. I remembered always having to attend Sunday mass, with Father O'Malley standing in front of the church wearing his fancy white Alb along with his fancy Amice with its detailed gold and red embroidery throughout the front and back. He always made sure we looked presentable as well. Being altar boys, we too were required to wear the white linen cassock. Even though Father O'Malley wasn't the Pope, he always made us kiss his ring, which he told us was a sign of respect to St. Vincent's for his services. Even now, I knew that was a bunch of BS. It was his way of showing that he had control over his church.

To me, he didn't mean anything, nor did he have any significant place in society as far as I was concerned. Pushing my feelings aside, I concentrated on the road. It wasn't hard to miss the old church as it sat between the tall buildings. If I hadn't known better, it looked more like a government building than a church with its tall concrete pillars and steep steps that led to the entrance. Parking my Tundra around the corner, I got out and headed up the stairs to where three large doors were. Choosing the one in the middle, I pulled open the heavy wooden door and stepped inside. The inside was more beautiful than I had imagined. Just past the narthex, the chapel doors were open, leading to an amazing place of worship. It had a row of stained-glass windows on each side of the room and a walkway which split the pews. The walls were painted in white, giving it a holy and sacred aura. The ceiling was high, with beautifully painted murals of Jesus' Crucifixion as well as different scenes depicting the Bible throughout the chapel.

As I was taking in the surroundings, a man came into view, which I knew was a priest based on his dress. Stepping up to him, I held out my hand and said, "Good afternoon, Father. My name is Lou Gainer. I understand that you have an induction of a new member of the clergy taking place this Sunday."

"That is correct. Brother Samuel will be taking over St. Peter's. I have given forty wonderful years to this church. It is going to be hard to leave," he explained as we began walking towards the alter. "Will you be attending the ceremony?"

"I wouldn't miss it. I understand that Father O'Malley will be among the assembly to ordain the new priest," I shared.

"He was supposed to be. Unfortunately, he will be unable to attend. He was called back to Chicago early this morning," the father remarked.

"That is unfortunate. Do you know why?" I questioned.

"An unforeseen incident at St. Vincent's. He is going to be missed," the priest confessed as he placed some additional candles on the tiered mantle where the lit prayer candles were.

As I left the church, at least now I knew that O'Malley wouldn't be attending the ceremony on Sunday. Getting in my truck, it was closely approaching one o'clock and I only had thirty minutes to get to the YMCA before my class started. As I started the engine, I couldn't get O'Malley off of my mind. Something had to be done. I was no longer that shy, scared boy from eighteen years ago. He needed to pay for what he did to me and so many others like me.

I will never forget about the boy whose bed was next to mine in the room where all of us slept. His name was Tommy Porter. I think of all of us, he was the most affected by what O'Malley did. Every time he was called away, I knew it was his turn to feed O'Malley's addiction. It seemed that he was always gone the longest. Sometimes he wouldn't show up until the next morning during breakfast. I always asked him if he was okay, but the only response I ever got was a blank stare. Come to think of it, he never said much of anything after his first encounter with that low-life motherfucker. Then one day he was gone. I wasn't sure what happened to him and none of the others knew either. When I asked Sister Claire, she told me that I needed to concentrate on taking care of myself and not worry about things that didn't concern me. To this day, I still think about him and wonder what happened to him. I kept hoping that he was placed with a good family. I even tried finding him when I left the orphanage and entered the service, but it was like he just disappeared. After several years of no luck, I stopped looking and convinced myself that he was doing well and living a good life.

Clearing my mind, I pulled away from the curb, heading to the YMCA where I knew twelve students would be waiting for me. These were the best kids ever. Some of them were from broken families and some were not so lucky to even have a family. It didn't matter what family life they had, I treated them all equally. I wanted them to learn discipline that would carry them through life. Martial arts was the only thing that got me through my earlier years, and I wanted these kids to learn this technique so they too would make it through life.

~****~

"Good afternoon, Sensei Gainer," they all said together.

"Good afternoon, class. Please take your places," I replied, waiting for each of them to find their spot.

Walking them through the first round of warm-ups, I settled on the mat and began doing my own warm-up, which consisted of a relaxing breathing technique known as Qigong. This was the only technique I found to help me clear my mind and body of everything. As I took in deep breaths, my efforts were stopped as I heard laughter coming from the back row. When I opened my eyes, the laughter immediately stopped, and silence once again filled the space, allowing me to return my focus on my breathing. It was funny knowing that I had such control over my students that just my gaze could cause them to pay attention.

The kids knew that my heart wasn't in the class today, just by the way it bounced off on them. This was the first time that I had lost all concentration. The only thing I could think about was what happened to me at that orphanage. I also kept thinking about all these kids. I wasn't any older than they were. To have your childhood taken away like mine was, was unforgivable.

Looking to the kids, I decided to call one of my top kids to head the class with instruction, while I pulled my head out of my ass and cleared my mind. The only way I knew to do that was to get rid of this anger that was building up inside me. A few rounds with the stationary kicking bag was just what I needed to release some of this tension.

CHAPTER FOUR
Emma

Finishing my snack, which consisted of a bag of chips, a candy bar, and a soda, I decided to do something for myself. Grabbing a few bills from my bag, I headed down the street to Fifth Avenue. It was so nice to finally have money of my own, even though technically it wasn't really mine. Most everything that I made at the Park Lane Hotel went to Red Oak Nursing Home where my mom had been staying for the past eight years. It was also the last time that I had seen her, but I always made sure that every penny I made went to the home to cover her monthly living expenses. The cheapest and the closest place I could find was in Illinois. As much as I hated not being able to visit her, I knew she was being well taken care of. And even though I couldn't see her, I checked in with the staff every week to make sure she was doing okay. Sometimes, I would sneak a call using the hotel phone, or Courtney would let me use her cell phone when she was working the same shift as me.

As much as I loved my mom, I hated her too. Growing up, the only thing that she cared about was where her next fix was going to come from. She did some pretty shady things while I was growing up in order to get it. I always wondered what our lives would have been like if she never started taking the stuff. At first it was just to deliver it, then she started using it herself. That was pretty much how she ended up in the nursing home. Her deliveries came up short one too many times and she ended up paying for it. Now, she doesn't even know her name half the time. She certainly doesn't know me or that I ever existed.

Standing in front of Saks Fifth Avenue, I decided this was as good a place as any to pick out something nice for myself. The minute I stepped into the fancy store, I knew that I was totally out of place Looking down at my weathered jeans and faded t-shirt, an embarrassment came over me as I tried to seem small, hoping no one would notice me. Walking quickly in between some mannequins. I was definitely in the wrong place. This store was too ritzy for me. Getting to the entrance door, I exited, hoping that no one noticed me.

Walking down the block, I slipped inside another store. As I was looking around, a sales associate started walking towards me. I pretended to be looking at some clothes on a rack when she began rambling about this sale and that sale. Nodding my head as though I heard everything she said, I smiled and said, "Thank you," before heading in the opposite direction.

When she was out of sight, I began to proceed to another section, where I spotted a cute little dress. As I pulled it off of the rack, I tried to think back to the last time I even wore a dress other than my uniform. Needless to say, I came up empty. Pulling the price tag from inside the back of the dress, I looked at it and was pleasantly surprised to find that it wasn't that much, at least not as much as I thought it would be. Heading back to the sales associate, I asked her politely for directions to the changing room.

Once inside, I stripped off my clothes and put on the dress. As I turned toward the mirror, I couldn't believe that it was me that I saw in the mirror. The dress fit perfectly and besides the worn tennis shoes on my feet, I had to admit that I looked pretty amazing. Turning this way and that way, I saw the dress really hugged my body, showing off curves I never knew I had.

I ended up spending a little bit more than I had planned, but at least I had a few nice things. Leaving the store with several bags, I was too tired to walk back to the motel with my purchases. Hailing a cab, I got in and told the driver where to go. Looking out the window, I saw a familiar face exit a high-rise apartment building. "Wow," I said out loud, causing the driver to look back to me in the review mirror.

"Is everything okay, Miss?" he asked with a hint of concern.

"Yes, I'm fine," I replied.

I had no idea that the guy I had met in the park earlier would be living in such a ritzy place. Pulling my bags closer to my body, I thought about how nice it would be to have a place that I could call mine. I knew that with the money I intended on keeping, I could have a nice place and get off of the street. It was then that I decided to look for a place as soon as I got back to the hotel. Maybe I was a little quick to think about returning all but a couple thousand dollars. If I kept it all, I could be happy a lot longer, instead of only a couple of months.

~****~

I stayed up later than I should have the night before, and my body was feeling the effects of it as I stumbled out of bed and headed to the bathroom, where I knew a quick shower would wake up this tired body. Taking off my t-shirt and panties, I turned on the faucet to the shower and began brushing my teeth while the water warmed up. Gazing up at the mirror, the lack of sleep could be seen by the dark circles under my eyes. Rinsing the toothpaste from my mouth, I inspected my teeth, making sure they were gleaming white with no food particles lingering between them. Even though I didn't have the best eating habits and knew that my body was lacking the nutrients it needed, I always made sure that my teeth remained healthy by brushing them and flossing whenever I had a chance.

As the warmth of the water cascaded down my body, I couldn't believe how wonderful it felt. Taking the white washcloth, I rubbed the bar of soap against the dampened cloth until a good layer of suds appeared on it. Rubbing the cloth against by body, I closed my eyes and began thinking about Lou. I wasn't sure why, but there was something about him that filled my mind. Even though I had never been with a man or even knew what it felt like to be kissed by one, all I could think about was how it would feel to be with him.

Lowering the soapy cloth down my body, I reached the apex of my sex. Sliding it between my legs, I closed my eyes and began imagining that it was Lou touching me, caressing me. Unable to get the satisfaction I needed from the cloth, I let it drop to the bottom of the tub and put my hand in its place. With my middle finger, I gently parted my folds and began moving it slowly back and forth. The moisture between my legs began to build as my finger began moving more freely. With my other hand, I pinched my nipple between my fingers, pulling and tugging on the hard peak, just enough to cause my nipple to tingle with excitement. Seeing Lou's hands caressing my body sent a surge of rhapsody through my veins and just the thought of him sent me reeling. As I increased my movements, my body unleashed. Feeling the last tremble wash through me, my body began to relax with only the disappointment that it was not the touch of his hands upon me, but my own. I had never had the desire to be with any man, so why was Lou any different, and why did I feel the need to feel him touch me?

Coming back to reality, I finished drying off and put on my neatly pressed uniform. Combing my long hair, I grabbed a hair-tie and pulled it back into a ponytail. As I looked in the mirror at my reflection, I could see that my complexion was a little bit flushed, most likely due to the self-indulgence I had in the shower. Normally I would nix the make-up, but I wanted to look my best in the event I ran into Lou again on my way to and from work. Since I knew exactly where he lived, or at least the building he lived in, I decided to take the scenic route to work.

Picking up my bag, I placed in on the bed. The last thing I wanted was to risk getting caught with all this money. Looking around the room to find a good place to hide it, I remembered seeing an old safe hidden away in one of the cupboards. I wasn't sure if it even worked. Reading the directions that were affixed to the door, I punched in a four-digit code and pressed the lock button. Pulling on the handle to make sure it was secure, I re-entered the code to open it. At least now I knew that my money would be safely tucked away.

After placing the last bundle in the safe, I headed out the door and down the street. It was still pretty early in the morning to be walking, but I was no stranger to the streets. It never bothered me to walk alone when it was dark. The only thing good about living on the streets was that I learned how to take care of myself if anyone entered my space. Seeing as how this was a better part of the city, I felt pretty confident that I would be safe.

Looking up to the building where I saw Lou exit, I imagined which apartment was his and what he would be doing at this very minute. Lost in thought, I didn't realize that I had stepped off the sidewalk and into the street until an annoying honk broke me from my fantasy. Stepping back onto the sidewalk, I heard the driver yell, "Get off the fucking street. Next time I'll run your ass over."

Giving him a sideways glance, I lifted my hands and gave him a double bird as my response. Another thing I learned living on the streets, never put up with any shit. Continuing on my way, I crossed the street and headed into Central Park. One of the places I most hated walking through in the dark was the park at night. There were so many greedy homeless people who slept here at night, just waiting until the night patrolmen kicked them out. A lot of them I knew, but the ones I didn't tended to hide among the bushes to stay out of sight. When a passer-by came close to them, they found it a good opportunity to beg for food, among other things. I knew this all too well, being that I used to be one of those people.

Walking on the sidewalk, there were only a few people out this early in the morning. Most of them were doing their morning run. One thing that was nice about working at the Park Lane Hotel was that it was within walking distance of the park. Sometimes, I would even walk to the park and just sit on one of the benches overlooking the water on Turtle Pond. They say that if you go to the top of Belvedere Castle and look out, you can see the turtles in the water. I have never seen them since I could never afford to get inside the castle to find out.

As I entered the hotel, just like usual, the place was already beginning to come alive. Already one of the other hotel maids had been busy dusting the furniture, while another one was mopping the shiny floors. Slipping past the check-in desk, I noticed a couple of men who looked like they pumped one too many irons standing next to the elevators, as well as the staircase. I brushed it off and headed to the wooden door that led to the employee area where the employee lockers were, and the head of housekeeping office.

Opening my locker to stash my bag away, I overheard one of the girls talking to another. From what I could hear, they were talking about the incident that happened yesterday. Seems that one of the guests staying in a Junior Suite had been shot. I couldn't hear all the details, but I knew when money was mentioned in the conversation, it had to be the same room that I helped Courtney clean. Unable to control my curiosity, I closed my locker and walked up to the two girls.

"So, it was pretty exciting here yesterday. I always miss out on all the fun," I remarked, interrupting their conversation, hoping that they would say more about what happened.

"Yeah, it was pretty exciting. Some guy in the Junior suite on the 46th floor got toasted. They found some bundled hundred dollar bills all over the floor. We can't even clean the room until they are done collecting the evidence. I guess they were checking everything for prints, even the money," one girl confessed as she wrapped her apron around her waist and tied it in the back.

When the girl said, "Catch you later," it didn't register until she was out the door. My heart sunk to the pit of my stomach. All these thoughts began running through my mind. *"I touched that damn money. My prints would be on those bills."* I felt like I was going to be sick. Walking back to my locker, I entered my combination and removed the lock. Grabbing the bottle of water that I tucked in my bag, I took a long drink. I only wished there was something stronger in my bag that I could drink.

Leaving the employee lockers with my stocked maid's cart, I knew I needed to get my head straight. The last thing that I needed was for someone to notice that I was acting strange. Taking in a deep breath, I took the clipboard with my cleaning schedule, which was tucked between two piles of freshly washed towels. Scanning the pages, I headed to the service elevator and punched in the 30th floor. One good thing about working at the hotel was that Delores, who was the head of housekeeping, always made sure that the cleaning schedules were different every day. She felt that having a different schedule daily helped with the morale and the boredom that came with cleaning the same rooms every day. Personally, I think she did it to find out who was doing a better job at cleaning the rooms. Even though we never saw the reviews left by the guests, she always made sure we knew if there were any bad ones by giving us the shittiest jobs.

Exiting the elevator, I pushed my cart to the first room. Once again, I noticed a he-man standing just down the hall from the staircase. I wasn't sure what was going on, but I had a feeling it had to do with the guy that was killed. As I swiped my card to enter the room, I heard my pager go off.

Pulling it from my pocket, I could see that the number for housekeeping was displayed. Walking through the door, I headed for the telephone, which was sitting on the desk near the unmade king-sized bed. Pushing the housekeeping button on the panel, I waited for someone to answer.

"Housekeeping, this is Heather. How can I assist you?" she asked in a cheery voice.

"Hi, Heather. This is Emma. I was paged," I replied, wondering what could be the reason.

"Hold on, Emma. Let me find out who paged you."

Holding the receiver to my ear, I looked out the large window that overlooked Central Park. It was still very early and the sun was barely beginning to come up. As I waited, I began to wonder if Lou was out there somewhere doing his morning jog. Turning away from the window, I began straightening the magazines that were scattered across the glass coffee table in front of the white velvet couch.

"Emma, hi... it's Delores. I need you to stop by my office before you leave for the day," Delores advised.

"Is there a problem, Delores?" I asked, concerned.

"No, no… nothing like that. I'll see you then."

Before I could quiz her any further, the line went dead. Hanging up the receiver, I headed back to the room's door to gather the things I needed to begin cleaning the room. While I was cleaning, I kept wondering why Delores needed to see me. Even though she admitted that there wasn't a problem, I knew that she was good at keeping things from us. Only on very rare occasions did she ever have our back. She could be a bitch at times, but when she wanted something she would become your best friend. I remembered the time that she wanted us to keep an eye on the gentleman who was staying in the penthouse suite for a couple of weeks while he was in the city for a meeting with some hotshots. I think she wanted to get her claws into him. It was just him that was staying in the penthouse and he wasn't wearing a wedding ring, which, according to Delores, made him free game.

Delores wasn't ugly by any means. She was actually quite attractive. Even though she kept her hair pulled back, I could tell it was gorgeous. It was a deep brown and fell to the middle of her back. She had blue eyes that were just as gorgeous as her hair. She wasn't skinny, but she carried her larger frame elegantly. There was no end to the number of curves she had. But if there was one thing that set all of those enticing features to the wayside, it was her temper. I learned long ago never get on her bad side. She was definitely the kind of person that could make your life a living hell.

I will never forget how angry she got when she found out that the handsome man in the penthouse suite was actually married, and to top it off, a cheater. When he had asked her to join him for a drink, Delores thought for sure she had found her Prince Charming. He was a charmer all right. Charmed her right into his bed, and then he went straight out the door, right after he told her, "Thanks, it was fun." I really couldn't blame her for being pissed, but to take it out on her staff was just wrong.

After I finished cleaning the last of the rooms on my schedule, I got onto the service elevator to head down to Delores' office. Even though my day went by in a blink, I was glad to get it over and find out what she needed to see me about. After re-stocking my cart and taking the soiled linens to the laundry, I headed to her office. I could see that she had someone in there and I wasn't sure if she wanted to be disturbed. Since her door was shut, I lightly knocked on it. When she gave me the okay to enter, I opened the door.

Sitting in one of the chairs adjacent to her desk was Lou. My face tightened as my teeth clenched together. Perturbed that he showed up where I worked, I could only wonder what the hell he was doing here.

CHAPTER FIVE
Gainer

The look on Emma's face was indescribable. I couldn't tell if she was pissed off or just plain surprised to see me. Needing to put an end to her agony, I stood from my seat and held out my hand.

"Hi. My name is Lou Gainer, but everyone calls me Gainer. I work for Jagged Edge Security. Please have a seat while I go over some things with you," I said, giving her a smile while I waited for her to shake my hand, which unfortunately didn't come.

"Delores, what is this about?" Emma asked, refusing to take a seat next to me.

"Emma, please take a seat. Mr. Gainer will explain everything," Deloris commanded.

When Emma finally gave in and took a seat, I could almost feel the heat from her anger radiate towards me.

Turning my head her way, I tried to get her attention. "Emma, as you may or may not know, there was an unfortunate incident yesterday in one of the suites. Ms. Tucker, Delores, has agreed to allow us to get a handle on what may have happened to the gentleman staying in the suite. The hotel manager has requested additional security and we want to make sure we provide the best service that Jagged Edge Security possibly can. But in order to do that, we need to find out as much information as possible."

"I don't know what this has to do with me. I only learned this morning, from one of the girls, that a guy got whacked," Emma responded.

"Well... since you were in the room with another maid cleaning, we thought you could let us know if there was anything weird about the room, or if you may have found something while you were cleaning," I asked, hoping she would be able to help us out.

"I didn't see anything. Can I please go? I have somewhere that I need to be," Emma retorted as she stood from her seat, heading towards the door.

Knowing that there was more to her story just by her abrupt answer, I stood as well and said, "I need to get going as well. I'll be in touch, Delores."

Emma must have ran as fast as she could out of the employee area, because when I opened the door to the hallway that led to the lobby, she was nowhere in sight. Taking a chance, I headed towards the front doors of the hotel, hoping that I would catch her leaving. Just as I got to the lobby area, I caught a glimpse of her going out the glass doors and heading to her right. Walking as fast as I could without causing a scene, I headed out the door and down the sidewalk. It was late enough in the morning that the sidewalk was already crowded with pedestrians, presumably taking an early lunch

Weaving in and out of the bodies, I finally spotted her up the street waiting for the light to change so that she could cross it. I was just about ready to yell her name, but thought better. I didn't want to chance her running off. Increasing my stride, I was able to catch up to her before the light changed.

"Emma, wait up," I shouted.

Her eyes were drawn to my voice and she held her ground as I continued to approach her. Running my hands through my hair, I looked down on her and asked, "Why did you leave so fast?"

"I don't know what you want from me. Even though I helped Courtney clean that room, I didn't notice anything." Her tone was high-pitched and I knew that she wasn't being totally honest.

"It's okay, Emma. I was just going to ask if you wanted to grab something to eat," I said, trying to get her to calm down.

"I'm sorry, I can't. With everything going on, we have been hit hard at work. I'm exhausted and just want to relax. Do you know how hard it is to work around the added security?"

"Well, at least let me walk you home?" I offered.

"No! I mean, I can make it on my own."

"What is going on with you, Emma? You seemed to be on edge."

"I am, maybe just a little," she began, stopping and turning towards me. "I have a lot going on."

"Let me walk you home, Emma. We can talk about it. I am a good listener."

"Okay, but you have to promise not to judge me when you see where I am currently staying."

"I never judge, Emma," I confessed, placing my hand on her cheek to reassure her it didn't matter. Even if she lived in a box, I would still want to get to know her.

As we headed towards the park, I couldn't help but look down at her. She was the most gorgeous woman I had ever laid eyes on. Even with her hair pulled back and minimal make-up on, she was breathtaking. I could only imagine what she would look like with her silky brown hair, which was the color of dark chocolate, cascading down her velvety soft skin. All I could think about was how it would feel to touch her, to feel her body next to mine. My thoughts were interrupted when a man, not watching where he was going, bumped into Emma and nearly knocked her over. Holding on to her so that she didn't topple over, I steadied her and asked, "Are you okay?"

With annoyance, she responded, "What a jerk," as she took hold of her arm.

It was only then that I noticed that she was bleeding. "Emma, your arm."

As she looked down at her arm, something changed in her. Her face grew pale and she began to wobble back and forth. Before I could say anything, my arms were around her. I wasn't sure what had just happened, but I knew I needed to do something. Since we were just across the street from my place, and I wasn't sure where she lived, I scooped her up and began heading in the direction of my apartment.

~****~

When I got inside my building, I quickly punched the up button on the elevator panel and waited for it to arrive. Emma began stirring in my arms, which told me that she beginning to wake up. I wasn't sure what would have caused her to go out like that, but I wasn't going to give up finding out.

Opening the door to my apartment, I carefully maneuvered her through the door, kicking it closed with my foot once we were inside. Carrying her over to the leather couch, I gently placed her on it and began inspecting her arm. Looking at the cut, I could tell it wasn't too deep and wouldn't need stiches. All she really needed was a couple of bandages to keep the cut together and help with the bleeding. I made sure she was comfortable before heading to the bathroom to see what I could find to doctor her cut.

Everything I needed was in a first-aid kit that I keep in the bathroom cupboard. When I headed back to the living room, Emma was still in the same position that I had left her in. As I took my time to mend her wound, her eyes began to flutter open. I could tell by the way she was looking at me that she was a little confused by what was going on

Easing her confusion, I cupped her cheek and said softly, "You passed out in the park after some guy cut you. Do you know who he was?"

"I don't think so. All I can remember is walking, and then a man bumping into me. Then the blood. So red. The smell," Emma explained as her mind began to wonder somewhere else other than here.

"Emma," I shot out to bring her back. "Where did you go?"

"I hate blood. Ever since I was a little girl, just the sight of it made me pass out. I guess some things will never change," she confessed.

"Did something happened to you when you were young to cause you to keel over like that?" I quizzed.

"I don't remember. All I know is that just the sight of it makes me sick enough to pass out."

"Well, I have an idea. I mean… since you are already here. How about I order us something to eat and we can hang out together for a while?" I suggested.

As she settled back, I gently rubbed her cheek with my thumb. I wasn't sure what got into me, but I moved closer to her and captured her lips with mine. Her lips slowly parted, giving me the access I needed to explore the depths of her warmth. It was a little awkward at first, but then she began to mimic my movements and it was like going to heaven. When her arms wrapped around my shoulders, I could no longer hold back. She was delicate and naive. I knew this just by the way she responded to the kiss. But now was not the time to call her on it.

Lifting her from the couch, I placed her on my lap as I continued my play with her lips. They were silky soft, like the petals of a rose. I reached behind her and untied the bow to her apron so I could gain access to the double row of buttons down the front of her uniform. Pulling the apron away, my mouth was still tied to hers as I began undoing each button, one by one. I thought I would finally be able to feel her soft skin next to mine when my efforts were stopped as she placed her hand over mine. I didn't want this to end, but I also didn't want her to feel uncomfortable. "It's okay, Emma, I will never do what you don't want me to. But I have a feeling you want this as much as I do," I confessed in a heated breath as her hand left mine and ended up around my neck.

I could feel the strength of her arms tighten around my shoulders as she pulled me closer. Having the buttons to her uniform undone, I glided my hand beneath the front of her dress and slowly caressed her body. Our lips reconnected to each other like a magnetic force as soon as her dress was lifted away. I could finally see what I had been fantasizing about. Even though her dress was still on and all I could see were her ample breasts covered by her modest bra, the shape of her breasts was perfect. I knew that my touch was having an effect on her by the way her nipples peaked through the thin material of her bra.

As much as I wanted her, this was not the place to take her. Standing from the couch, holding her tightly to my body, I lifted her and began walking with her to my bedroom, where I knew she would be more comfortable. The minute I took the first step, her lips pulled away from mine and the look on her face told me that I had messed up. Standing silently still, I could barely hear her words as she said, "I've never been with anyone."

Thinking that I may have misunderstood her, I asked in a soft voice, "No one, ever?" continuing my exploration of her body, placing soft kisses along her neck and shoulder.

When she didn't answer, I stopped and looked at her. I could have sworn that tears were about to fall from her eyes. Her head began moving back and forth letting me know that she had never been with a man before. This was something that I wasn't prepared for. As much as I wanted her, I knew that this was a very delicate situation and I wasn't sure if I was the right man to show her.

Placing her on her feet. I held her close to my body and said softly, "I would never do anything you weren't comfortable with. We will take this as slow as you need to."

Placing my hand on her cheek, I lowered my head and gently kissed her on the lips. It was as if they were meant to be a part of me. Her hands wrapped around my neck as she pushed to her tippy-toes in order to pull me closer. Taking hold of her firm ass, I lifted her from the floor and held her tightly as I walked with her to my room while consuming every inch of her warm mouth. Out tongues collided together, sending a surge of pleasure down to my aching arousal. Pressed to my body, I placed my hand on her back and guided her slowly down onto the bed.

The heat between us began to ignite as I pulled her dress away. I knew that if she didn't will me to stop, I would never be able to control myself. Raising my head to look down upon her, I move a stray piece of hair from her cheek and whispered intently, "Are you sure you want me to continue?"

The fire in her beautiful brown eyes said it all. I just wasn't sure if she was ready for what I was about to give her. Releasing the front clasp of her bra, the mounds of her femininity spilled out with her nipples greeting me with pure perfection. There was nothing more perfect. I gazed up at her to make sure she was still with me before lowering my head to her breast and capturing her taut nipple between my lips. Just the taste of her succulent scent made the bulge between my legs take over, consuming what little room I had left in my jeans.

Despite being no stranger to women, this might have been the first time that my body had reacted in this way. Seizing her other breast, I lowered my hand down her soft skin to her firm stomach until it came to rest just shy of the waistband to her white cotton panties. Flattening my hand against her warm skin, I worked to lower them as I slid my hand underneath the soft material of her panties. Feeling the heat radiate under my fingers, I knew that she wanted this as much, if not more than I did.

I could feel the slick wetness of her pussy as I nudged my finger between her velvety folds. Her hips began to move as I found her clit and began making circular movements on the swollen nub. I could feel the strength of her hands gripping my hair as I continued my assault on her swollen nub. Emma's back began to arch and a soft moan escaped her mouth, letting me know that the pleasure she was receiving was beginning to take hold. With gentle ease, I slipped a finger inside her tight channel. Her moans turned into whimpers, stopping me in my efforts. Tilting my head towards her face, I tried to determine if I might have been hurting her. Unable to see her expression, I asked in a low, calm voice, "Emma, are you okay, sweetheart?"

When there was no response, I repeated myself. "Emma, I need to know that you are okay."

"Yes, just a little surprised," she confessed as her breath hitched.

"Nice and slow, baby," I replied, continuing where I left off.

Pushing my finger further inside her tight channel, I curved it to just the right angle to make sure she would know what it felt like to come totally undone. When her whimper turned into a scream, I knew that she had reached her destination. Emma's body began to shudder with satisfaction. Satisfaction also hit me, knowing that I was the one who brought her so much pleasure.

CHAPTER SIX
Emma

Lying in Lou's bed, I couldn't wrap my head around how different I felt. How could just a single touch have me so confused? Being twenty-five, I realized just what I had missed. Experiencing the touch of a man was so much better than my own. For years, I never had the desire to be satisfied, other than by my own hand. I knew that a lot of it had to do with the life I was given and the fact that being with someone else was never an option for me. Most of the men that I had met on the street were either too old or too strung out on drugs to even care about anything except where they were going to get their next fix.

I do remember a young guy, about my age, that came around once in a while. He was kind of cute with his long hair that he always had pulled up in a man bun. I will never forget the color of his eyes, either. They were as blue as the sky on a clear day. I really never got the chance to know him. I only knew that he went by the name of TJ.

Pulling away from my thoughts, I wasn't sure what time it was, but I knew that I was starving. As I rolled over, Lou was still snoozing away. It was still light outside, so I knew it had to still be early in the afternoon. When I started pushing from the bed, Lou grabbed my arm before I could stand.

"Where are you going, baby?" he asked with his eyes slowing opening.

"I thought I would grab something to eat. I'm starving," I replied as I took in his features.

His body was bare from the waist up. At least that is what I assumed, since the rest of his body was covered with the sheet. I had never seen so many muscles on one guy in my life. Every ripple and curve of his chest and abs were like they were masterfully sculpted by Michelangelo. Lou must have noticed my fixation on his body, because I was no longer sitting on the bed, but pulled back just enough so that he was now hovering over me. When our eyes met, my hunger for food went away, leaving me craving only him. Lou gently placed his lips on mine. While I was thinking that he was going to pleasure me again, the kiss was over before it began. Feeling deprived, I watched as he slipped his t-shirt over his head. He was still wearing his jeans, which meant that even though I was naked, aside from my white plain-Jane panties, I didn't feel uncomfortable. This was also a first for me. I had never exposed my body to anyone. Not even the other ladies at the shelter got a glimpse of me, despite the fact that we had to share the bathroom.

Grabbing my bra that had somehow ended up on the floor, I didn't say a word. Slipping it on and hooking the front clasp, I found my uniform dress and began pulling it over my legs. As I stood buttoning the top button, I was able to take in my surroundings. Lou's room was a typical male room, with a bike parked in one corner. It was actually pretty clean for a man's room. The furniture was new and dark. All of the pieces matched, which told me that it must have cost him a pretty penny. As I continued to look around I could see that there was a bathroom within the room.

Doing up the last button on my dress, I looked over to where Lou was standing and asked softly, "Is there a bathroom I can use?"

Pointing to the door that was partially open, he replied, "Yeah, you can use this one. I'm going to see what I can find to order. Is there anything special that you like?"

Stopping in my tracks, I turned my head, not looking at him, and said, "I can't stay. I need to get going."

"I thought you said you were hungry."

"Not anymore," I replied as I headed to the bathroom and closed the door, leaving him to ponder my response.

Even though I was starving, I couldn't spend any more time with Lou. As much as I wanted to, there was no way I could risk him learning more about me.

~****~

I didn't know how I managed to do it, but I was able to convince Lou that he didn't need to walk me to my motel. Maybe it was the fact that I was no more than a few blocks from him. He, of course, didn't know this, but when I said, "The motel isn't far," he let it go. The only thing that I wanted to do was try and find a place near the Park Lane Hotel. Something fully furnished would be good.

When I dug in the pocket of my uniform to pull out my key, I came up empty. The only thing that I could think of was that it must have fallen out at the park when I collapsed. Turning on my heels, I headed to the motel office to request another key. Just like the Park Lane Hotel, I knew that it wouldn't be a big deal to code another key card so that I could gain access to my room.

After the gentleman at the front desk was kind enough to give me a new key, I headed back to my room to shower and then begin my search for a new place to live. As I was walking up the steps to my room, I had this sudden chill down my body. It was like someone was watching me or following me. When I peered over the balcony leading to my room, there was a young guy standing below me. I recognized him immediately.

Leaning over the edge of the iron rail, I said loudly so the guy could hear, "Hey, you."

When he looked up at me, it was him, the guy from the streets by the name of TJ. I thought for sure he was long gone. He actually looked pretty good for a homeless person. I hadn't seen him for several months. It made me wonder what he had been up to during that time. Heading back in the direction of the steps, I gazed down on him as he began walking in the same direction. By the time I got to the steps, he was already waiting for me at the base. As I descended the steps, his eyes were upon me with each step I took. Standing on the bottom step, I smiled up at him and asked, "It's been a long time. How have you been?"

The more I thought about it, the more it occurred to me that I hadn't seen TJ for more than eight months, and now he was here. How the heck could that be unless he had been following me? Not waiting for him to answer, I answered for him. "Wait, I know exactly how you have been. Have you been following me?"

"It's not like that," he replied.

"So, you can actually talk. All that time we were under that bridge, not once did you ever talk to me. So why are you here now?" I asked, needing answers that better be good, because following someone was just wrong.

"I saw you in the park with that guy. It wasn't like I was stalking you. I just wanted to catch up. You were the only person who was nice to me from the streets. So, I followed you," he explained.

Thinking that he was telling me the truth, I smiled at him. "Do you want to come up to my room? We could catch up there, or would you rather go to the coffee shop around the corner?" I didn't know what made me offer to go to my room. Even though we spent time together under the bridge, I had no clue what he really was like. For all I knew he could be a really bad person.

"Your room is fine, unless you would rather go to the coffee shop."

As I headed up the steps with TJ following behind, I began to wonder what it was that he really wanted. It didn't look like he was hurting for money. Matter of fact, it looked like he had done well for himself. I could tell by the way he was dressed that he spared no expense on his clothing. Reaching my room, I swiped my key card and turned the handle. Entering the room first, I slung my bag on the bed and waited for TJ to close the door and take a seat. I could tell that he had a lot on his mind. Taking a seat on the bed, I was about to say something when he began.

"So, it looks as though you made it off the streets," he said.

"Yeah, I guess you could say that. Looks like you've done pretty good as well," I replied.

"Yeah, I just couldn't stand living on the streets anymore. I knew that if I didn't do something, I was going to die there. So, with the little money I had, I bought some clean clothes and began searching for a job. Come to find out, I was really good at solving problems. Got a job at one of those call centers where people call in for help. Now I'm the day manager, and making enough money and then some." TJ paused before beginning again. "How about you? What are you doing now?"

"I work at the Park Lane Hotel as a maid. Even though it isn't as prestigious as your job, I've been able to save some money to help out my mom, plus stay off the street."

One thing I didn't tell him was that the additional money I came into was a big part of it. That was something no one was ever going to find out. Seeing that the cupboard was still open from earlier, I walked over to it casually and pushed it shut. Continuing our conversation, we talked about growing up and how he was brought up in an orphanage and couldn't stand it there anymore and ended up on the streets. TJ already knew about my past and the situation my mom left me in, so there wasn't very much that he didn't know.

Before he left, he handed me a small piece of paper with his cell number on it, requesting that we keep in touch. Taking the number from him, I knew then that the first thing I needed to do was get a cell phone of my own. Waiting just long enough for him to leave, I walked over to the safe and grabbed a few bills. Stuffing them in my pocket along with my key, my mind was set on finding a place where I could get a cell phone.

Heading down Madison, I spotted an electronics store where I knew they would have cell phones. Once inside the small store, I began searching for where the phones would be. Standing behind the counter that held an assortment of phones, a young guy was playing on his own cell. Getting his attention, I cleared my throat and asked, "Do you by chance sell reasonably priced cell phones that I could use for talking and texting?"

"Yes, Ma'am," he smiled, placing his cell in his pocket.

As he showed me different designs and features on cells, my mind was jumbled with information that it couldn't possibly hold. Stopping the man before he showed me another phone, I said, frustrated and confused, "I really don't need anything fancy. All I want is a simple phone that I can make calls or texts from. Nothing more."

When I finally left the electronics store, I left with a cell phone with no added features which came with a two-year contract costing me thirty dollars a month. My one and only contact was the nursing home where my mother was being kept, which the young guy graciously entered into my phone for me. As soon as I got back to the hotel I would be entering TJ's number, giving me two contact numbers.

The first thing I did when I got back to my room was call Red Oaks Nursing Home to check on my mom. Waiting for someone to pick up the phone, I sat at the small table and began once again flipping through the classifieds to find a place to live. Hearing the lady on the other end greet me with, "Red Oaks Nursing Home, how may I help you?" I waited patiently until she finished.

Taking a deep breath, hoping that this would be the day my mom would be able to speak with me, I asked confidently, "Can you please transfer me to Carolyn Atwood's room?"

"Hold on. Let me make sure she's in her room," the lady responded.

Just when I was thinking she might have forgotten about me, she came back and said, "I'll transfer you now."

Even though there was no response on the other end, I could hear the sound of my mom's breath on the other end. "Mom, it's Emma. Are you there?"

"Do I know you?" she asked in a shallow tone.

"Yes, Mom. I'm your daughter, Emma."

"Why would you say that? I don't have a daughter. She died before she was even born."

"Mom, it's me, Emma," I cried, trying to understand why she would think that I was dead. This was so much worse than before. At least before she knew me, even if it wasn't as her daughter.

"You are not my daughter. She's dead. Don't you ever call me again."

Before I could say another word, the line went dead. As I stared at the cell, I just couldn't bring myself to dial the number again. All I could think about was curling up into a small ball and dying. *How could this happen?* After waiting so long just to hear her voice, finding out that in her mind I didn't exist was beyond what I had expected. All I ever wanted was to have my mom back. But instead, I might have lost her forever.

CHAPTER SEVEN
Gainer

Letting Emma go so easily probably wasn't the best decision I had ever made. The minute she went through the door, I knew I should have stopped her, but then I held back thinking that this was going to be the best way to get her to open up to me. Looking out the living room window, I watched as she headed across the street and over to Central Park. I knew that she had to live close by, and it was about time I found out just where.

When I knew she was well out of sight, I slipped on my shoes, grabbed a shirt, and headed out of my apartment building to see if I could find out just where that somewhere might be. Crossing the street into the park's entrance, I became aware of my surroundings, hoping that I didn't wait too long to follow her. It was just then that I spotted her just over the bridge. Stopping, Emma rested her arms on the bridge wall and took a look over the edge. My guess was that she was stopping to admire the view.

As I watched her carefully from a safe distance, she began walking again, turning to her right once she was over the stone bridge. I really wasn't sure where she was headed, but I continued to follow her nonetheless. My only regret was that I couldn't get any closer to her without being seen. The way her hips moved with every step she took was enough to drive a man crazy. I was still amazed that she had never been with a man until me.

She soon exited the park and turned to her left, heading down Central Park West, where she crossed the street at 74th. I must have been following her for a good twenty minutes. If she lived in this vicinity, she had quite a commute on foot to the Park Lane Hotel. As she headed down the parking lot of a mediocre motel, I knew that she was at her destination. Keeping out of sight behind a tree, I watched her climb the only set of steps to the second floor of the motel. Now, not only did I know where she was living, but I also knew which room she was staying in.

While I waited until she got inside her room, she suddenly looked behind her as though she was waiting for someone to follow her. When she began nodding her head back and forth, I knew that she must have thought someone was behind her. Walking over to the balcony, Emma looked over the edge. Following her lead, I looked in the same direction to find that a man about my height, but with a smaller build, was standing below her looking up at her. Thinking that this guy might be a threat to her, I was just about ready to intervene when I could see that she was talking to the man and a smile came upon her face. I wasn't sure who this guy was, but I was going to find out.

I held back behind the tree for a moment longer until the man and Emma began walking towards her room. When they both entered, it was the perfect chance to see what the hell was going on. Making my way across the parking lot, I headed up the steps towards her room. Standing just outside her door, I put my ear to the wood and concentrated on the conversation that was going on inside. I could only hear bits and pieces of what they were talking about. The only thing that I could make out was that they knew each other from the bridge, which made absolutely no sense to me. I also got the impression from the conversation that the guy lost his mom and was placed in some sort of orphanage. I really couldn't give two shits about this guy. All I wanted was to know more about was Emma, but unfortunately nothing was said about her past. Evidently the guy already knew her pretty well, at least from what I could hear of their conversation.

Hearing enough, I thought it was best that I hightailed it out of there before I got caught. I didn't need Emma to find out that I had been spying on her. She was already pretty closed off and the last thing I needed was for that door to be locked for good.

~****~

After a long shower and grabbing a bagel with ham and cheese, I was on my way to the shop. On the way, the only thing I could think about was Emma and the guy she was talking to in her motel room. The way it sounded after being with her yesterday, she hadn't had any men friends, so it surprised me that she even knew any. This was something that I would need to bring up to her. I had to be very subtle with her or she would be suspicious of me knowing about her guest. I knew that I would be running into her sometime today, considering that Mike, Sly, and I were on security duty at the Park Lane Hotel. It would give me the chance to find out who he was.

~****~

We all decided to pile into Mike's 4-Runner and head on over to the hotel. As we were getting ready to head out,

Peter came out of the shop raising his hand, letting us know to hold up. I was riding shotgun so I rolled down my window to find out what was up. "What's up, Peter?" I asked, just as confused as my bros.

"The report came back on the money that was found in the dead guy's hotel room." Peter paused as we concentrated on what he was telling us. "The only prints they found were from the dead guy."

"Wouldn't it be our luck that there wouldn't be more on those bills," Mike hissed.

"Not so fast," Peter began, "There's something else about those bills. They were counterfeit, and pretty good ones at that. My guess is whomever killed that guy was after something much bigger, otherwise they would have taken the money. Maybe whoever it was knew the bills were fake."

"The police checked that room from top to bottom and there wasn't anything else of value there. Maybe we need to take a closer look at the employees of the hotel," Sly suggested.

"Those bills didn't just make themselves. Maybe the dead guy was smart enough to keep the plates in a safe place," I countered. "Maybe that is why he ended up dead."

"Either way, it wouldn't be a bad idea to keep a closer eye on the employees," Peter directed, making sure he made eye contact with each of us.

Rolling the window up, I began to wonder if someone from the hotel got their hands on the counterfeit plates or if they were even there. If they were there, it would have to be someone who had access to the room. Even though Emma had full access, I was pretty sure she didn't take them. I was a pretty good judge of character and she just didn't seem the type of person who would steal anything. And after speaking with Delores, it was pretty evident that Emma was one of her most trustworthy employees.

It was just after seven o'clock when we got to the Park Lane Hotel. As we stepped inside through the back entrance that the employees used, I looked over to where the Delores' office was to find that she was not inside. Walking over to the employee lounge where the lockers were also located, I decided that this was a good time as any to check the lockers, at least the ones that didn't have locks. Opening the unlocked doors, there was nothing of importance inside of them. Most of them were filled with snacks and extra uniforms. I would have to wait until Delores got in to check the remaining lockers. Hopefully the employees would cooperate and not demand a warrant to search their lockers.

Heading out the door to the lobby, I could see that the patrons of the hotel were already up and moving. Taking my place at the check-in desk, I simply scanned the area, anticipating anything out of the ordinary to happen. Unexpectedly, Emma entered the hotel carrying her bag close to her body. I hated to think about it, but the way she was carrying her bag, she certainly didn't want it to get away from her. Leaving my post, I walked toward her, hoping that I could somehow get the bag away from her.

Her beautiful brown eyes met mine and a smile spread across her face. "Hey," I said as I bent over and kissed her cheek.

"I guess the hotel still has added security," she said hesitantly, her smile vanishing.

"Yeah," I replied, looking down at her bag. "Let me carry that for you. It looks heavy."

"Thanks," she said, removing her bag from her shoulder and handing it over to me.

Slinging it over my shoulder, we walked together side by side to the hallway leading to the employee lounge. Shifting the bag slightly, I grabbed the door handle and pushed the door open, letting Emma enter first. By the weight of the bag, she was packing something heavy. I couldn't imagine what it could be. Walking to where the lockers were, Emma looked over her shoulder and said, "You can set my bag on the floor, I need to make a quick trip to the bathroom."

Talk about getting a break. Setting the bag on the floor, I waited until she was out of view before I checked out the contents. Given that the coast was clear, I pulled back the zipper that seemed to be somewhat broken and began riffling through the contents. I found that the only reason the bag was so heavy was because she was packing several cans of refried beans and soup. Shaking my head in disbelief, I zipped the bag up and went over to the water machine away from the bag. As much as I wanted to question her about the canned items in her bag, I knew I couldn't unless I wanted to rat myself out for checking out her stuff.

While I was sipping my water, Emma emerged from the bathroom and headed to her locker. Sauntering slowly towards her without a care, I stood just opposite of the locker so I could at least get a good look inside. From what I could see there wasn't much of anything inside: A couple of aprons, a pair of white tennis shoes, a brush, and some girly lotions and things. Convinced that there was nothing out of the ordinary inside, I downed the rest of my water and walked over to the small trash can beside the water machine to dispose of it. I felt better knowing that at least Emma was in the clear. Just like Delores had said, she was the model employee.

Hearing the back door to the hotel open, just the woman I needed to see stepped through. As she entered her office, I followed close behind, making sure to close the door behind me. The last thing I needed was for Emma to know what I was up too. Delores was behind her desk getting herself settled in while I was making myself comfortable in the chair in front of her desk. Before I got the chance to sit, her voice rang with annoyance. "Is there something I can help you with, Mr. Gainer? I have a very busy day today."

Clearing my throat, I said with authority, "Matter of fact, there is. I need to search all of the employee lockers and I need you to tell them it is mandatory that they be checked."

"I can't do that, Mr. Gainer. The random check on the lockers has already been done," she sneered.

"Well, you will need to let them know that because of the incident in the suite, it will need to be done again. I'm sure your employees will understand."

"I hope you know what you are asking, because unhappy employees are unproductive ones."

I could tell by Delores's demeanor, she was not very happy with my request. At least she was on board with what needed to be done. One thing I was grateful for was that she didn't ask why.

CHAPTER EIGHT
Emma

The minute I walked through the hotel door and saw Lou standing at the check-in desk, my chest got tight. Just the sight of him standing there had me all undone. The only thing I could do was pretend that the effect he was having on me was nothing. I found it very difficult to control the party that was going on between my legs. It was a sensation that I had never experienced before, at least not with any other man.

Meeting him in the middle of the lobby, he looked even more perfect the closer he got. The blue of his v-neck t-shirt made his eyes seem a deeper, richer gray, accentuating the dark blonde of his lashes. He was the perfect specimen of a man if ever there was one. Catching myself gawking at him, I didn't realize how mesmerized I was by his features until I handed him my bag.

When we entered the employee lounge, the only thing I wanted to do was get to the bathroom. I needed to compose myself and the only private place to do that away from Lou was in the bathroom. Locking the door, I headed to the sink to splash some water on my face. If I could see how flushed my cheeks were, there was no doubt that Lou could see it too. Taking deep breaths one right after the other, I calmed my body before I made my way back to the lounge area.

No sooner than I got to my locker, Lou was right there. All the calming techniques I did in the bathroom were a complete waste. With him so close to me, my body began to tingle all over again and I knew that in a matter of minutes my panties would be soaked. I couldn't have been happier or more disappointed when I heard the back door open and found that Delores had entered. Even though the tingling between my legs was subsiding, I missed the sensation it gave me.

Going about my daily duties to clear my mind of Lou, I made sure that my maid's cart was fully stocked before heading to the service elevator to begin my day. When I got to the twentieth floor, I could see that Courtney was already starting her day. Pushing my cart to the first room I was scheduled to clean, I decided to pop in the room she was cleaning to give her a quick "Hello."

Finding her in the bathroom, I knocked lightly on the door and waited for her to turn around. The last thing I wanted was to scare her. When she turned my way, I waved my hand and said, "Hey, you."

"Hey," she replied with a smile before turning her body completely. "I was just finishing up. Do you want to share cleaning rooms today? It would make the time fly faster."

"I'm there, hun," I said, turning to leave.

"Emma," I heard Courtney say behind me. "Me and a couple of the other girls are going out tonight for a couple of drinks. I would like you to come."

"I don't know, Courtney. I'm not much of an outer."

"Come on, Emma. It will be fun. We are all going to meet back here around eight."

"I'll think about it." Heading out the door, I gave her another quick wave good-bye.

I couldn't remember the last time I had been out. Come to think of it, I had never been out. I don't even think I had ever tasted alcohol. My life had to be the most boring life ever. Maybe it was time that I stepped it up a little and got out more. I had been so worried about making sure my mom was taken care of that I didn't even realize the things that I was missing out on. It was only yesterday that I had been kissed for the first time by a man.

~****~

Maybe I shouldn't have agreed to share cleaning the rooms with Courtney. The only thing she was able to talk about was how fun it was going to be tonight and I had better go. Having enough, I finally gave in and told her that I would go. I don't know what I was thinking. I didn't even have anything suitable to wear. I guessed I could spend a few dollars on a new outfit.

Gathering my things from my locker, it dawned on me that I hadn't run into Lou all day. The only thing I could think of as to why, was because he got called away on another job, or he was where I wasn't. After all, there were forty-six floors to this hotel, and he could have been on any one of them.

Knowing that I needed to hurry so that I would have enough time to shop for something nice to wear for the girl's night out, as Courtney called it, I quickly changed out of my uniform into something comfortable, grabbed a few bills, and left my room fifteen minutes later. As I headed down Central Park West, I decided to treat myself by going to one of the higher-priced shops. Since this was my first night out, I wanted to look good, and the only way to do that was to shop at a boutique instead of the second-hand store where I normally went.

Two hours later, I was back at the motel carrying three bags filled with a couple of outfits, two new pairs of shoes, and a few extra essentials. If I wanted to look good, I needed to feel good about myself as well. This meant that I was going to give myself a total makeover. Placing my bags on the bed. I went to the bathroom to fill the tub full of water and add some of the bath oil I had purchased. Removing my clothes, I looked at myself in the mirror, taking hold of my hair to decide whether or not putting it up would be an option for me. Holding my hair on top of my head, I decided that the best 'do' for me would be to leave it down. In the meantime,

I grabbed my hair tie and pulled it back to keep it from getting wet from the tub water.

Slipping into the warmth of the water, I could already feel the bath oils beginning to work on my body. I was glad that I chose to go with the cherry vanilla scent. The aroma from the combined scents filled the small room like I was outside smelling the cherry blossoms in the wind.

I could have remained in the tub for another hour, but I knew that if I wanted to look my best, it was going to take some work, and I was going to need the additional time to get it done. Grabbing a towel, I stepped out of the tub and wrapped it tightly around my body. While my body was still wrapped in the towel, I headed to the bed where I had left the vanilla-scented body cream. There wasn't one inch of my body that wasn't covered with this amazing scent. The lady at the make-up counter said that this body cream was the best cream on the market and it would make my skin soft and smooth.

After my body was covered thoroughly with the scented cream, I grabbed the few items I would need to begin my total makeover. Placing the items on the bathroom counter, I took a quick look at my face in the mirror and decided this was going to need the most help. Applying my makeup as best I could, I stepped back from the mirror and had to admit that I looked good. Matter of fact, I looked really good. It was amazing what a little eye shadow and lipstick could do to a woman's face.

Finishing the final touches on my hair, the only thing left for me to do was to get dressed. Pulling the deep purple dress that I had purchased from the bag, I carefully stepped into it and began working it up my body. The dress itself was a form-fitting one that gathered from the middle thigh all the way to the neckline. The bottom of the dress below the thigh was left in a frilly skirt that opened up as I made a circle. I didn't know that much about dresses, but the sales clerk at the boutique said it accentuated all of my curves. Whatever that meant.

Being that I had never worn heels before, the sales clerk suggested that I begin with a lower heel until I got used to walking in them. Deciding on a pair of black sateen sling backs with a small velvet bow, I slipped them onto my feet to finish my ensemble. Looking in the mirror as best I could to get the full picture of myself, I couldn't believe that I was standing before it. I looked more like a woman you would see in a fancy magazine than a woman who was a maid at a fancy hotel.

It was close to eight o'clock and if I wanted to be on time, I knew I had better get going. Pulling the list of services from the hotel's brochure, I found the number to the local taxi service and dialed the number. I could have walked to the hotel, but feeling a little bit wobbly in my new shoes, I didn't want to chance falling on my ass. When I hung up with the taxi service, I grabbed the little clutch that was a "must have" according to the sales clerk at the boutique and filled it with my compact for touch-ups, lipstick, my ID, and a few of the smaller bills I had left. Making sure the door to my room was locked, I attempted to walk in a ladylike manner. Trying my best to walk down the steps, I finally made it to the bottom without incident. I was finding that the more I walked the easier it became.

The taxi driver was already waiting for me in the motel parking lot. As soon as he saw me, he quickly got out from behind the wheel and rounded the front of the car and opened the back door for me. That was definitely a first. Never had a taxi driver given two shits about opening the door for me. Smiling up to him, I slid inside and said, "Thank you," on the way in.

I didn't know what was going on with me, but all of a sudden, I started feeling butterflies in my stomach. There was no reason for me to feel this way. It must have been the excitement of going out for the first time. It might even have been because none of the other girls had ever seen me made up like this and my nerves were beginning to have a heyday.

When we reached the hotel, I pulled out a ten-dollar bill to give to the driver, only he was out and ready to open my door before he could take it. With his hand held out, my only option was to allow him to assist me out of the car. I knew then if he so much as kissed it, he would have four boney knuckles up his nose. Fortunately for him, he forfeited the opportunity.

Paying him where he stood, I waited until he pulled away from the curb before I headed inside the Park Lane Hotel. The last thing I wanted was to have him assist me inside. With confidence, I began walking to the front door of the hotel. Opening the door, Courtney and three other maids that worked at the hotel were lounging in the seating area closest to the reservations desk. One of the girls I recognized as Heather, but the other two with Courtney were girls I hadn't seen before.

As I got closer to them, I waved and greeted them, saying, "Hi."

"Emma," Courtney began as she hugged me, "I'm so glad you're here. I was worried that you wouldn't come." Turning to the other girls she began introducing them one by one. "I think you already know Heather. Kate and Melissa, this is Emma."

"Nice to meet you, Emma," Kate said.

"Same here, Emma. Are you ready to have some fun?" Melissa said, shaking her hips in some sort of weird dance move.

"As ready as I'll ever be," I answered with a half-smile.

"You look terrific, by the way," Courtney chimed in.

"Thanks," I replied, tugging the hem of my dress.

As we all headed out of the hotel, Courtney mentioned that the place we were going to go wasn't far and that it would be better if we walked. Not wanting to seem like a fifth wheel, which technically I was, I fell behind the other girls and concentrated on walking in my heels. Turning down the block, I was glad to see that Courtney stopped and looked up at the marquee above the door that read '*Surge*' and said, "This is it, girls. Let the fun begin.

The inside of the place was dark, with a ceiling glittering with tiny white and blue lights. There was a gentleman standing just inside the door asking everyone who entered for their ID's. As I handed him mine, he looked down at me with a smile and said, "Enjoy your evening, gorgeous," before giving my ID back to me. I had never been called gorgeous before, so you could only imagine how red my face felt when Courtney and the other girls began giggling at his comment.

Heading further inside, Courtney was the first one at the bar, ordering five of something called "Red Headed Slut." I had no idea what it was, but when the bartender placed them in front of us as we lined up at the bar, they did have a really pretty color.

"One, Two, Three, down the hatch, bitches," Courtney yelled.

Watching the girls tip their heads back, I took note and did the same. As the concoction slid down my throat, I had to admit that it tasted pretty good. Good enough to have another. Ordering another round, I found out that Fridays were Ladies' Night here and all the shots were two for one. I was very much enjoying this thing called Ladies' Night. Placing our glasses on the bar, everyone followed Courtney to a high-top table large enough to seat five. As we each took our seats a waiter came by and another round of "Red Headed Sluts" were ordered.

It had been a long time since I had this much fun. Courtney was the life of the party. I didn't realize how funny she actually was. While we were sitting at our table, she was making funny comments about all the guys that came to our table to ask us to dance. Heather and Kate ended up dancing with two of the guys, while Courtney and Melissa preferred to dance with each other. I caught myself swaying to the music as I sat on my chair. Getting into the groove, I felt a light tap on my shoulder. Turning slightly to see who it was, I was surprised to see TJ standing behind me. He had a big smile on his face. I had never been so glad to see anyone. Standing to my feet, I felt the room begin to spin. I guess that last shot wasn't such a good idea. Thankfully, TJ was there to steady me.

When my head finally quit spinning like a merry-go-round, I wrapped my arms around his shoulders and slurred, "Hey, stranger. Long time no see."

"Emma, how much have you had to drink?" he asked, holding me upright.

"Just a few," I giggled, tipping my head back before saying, "Let's dance."

Grabbing TJ by the hand, I dragged him to the dance floor. I wasn't sure how I managed to make it there, but I did. There were so many people bumping into me as I began to dance that it was a surprise that I didn't fall right over. A couple of times I could feel TJ's arms wrap around my waist, moving my hips from side to side as he danced with me. Turning to face him, the music began to slow and he pulled me closer to his body. I rested my head on his shoulder and moved my body in sync with his. Even though I had never danced before, I felt comfortable with TJ. His moves were so smooth and slow that it was very easy to follow him. Lifting my head, I looked up to him and confessed, "I love the way you dance."

I wasn't sure what the connection between us was, but TJ lowered his head and before I could object, his lips were on mine. My head was spinning as his tongue slowly began working its way inside my mouth. Under normal circumstances, I would have been able to resist what was taking place, but the mixture of alcohol and the fact that I felt comfortable with TJ took the last bit of resistance I had.

The moment was soon taken away when our connection was broken. Opening my eyes, what seemed like a heat of the moment kind of thing just turned into something much worse. Guilt began to settle in as I watched Lou grab TJ by the neck and literally drag him off the dance floor. Standing, completely dumbfounded, I was finally able to move as I began following Lou and TJ to back of the bar. When Lou pushed open the back door, I knew that I needed to get to them as soon as possible before something very bad happened.

Doing the best I could, I tried pulling Lou off of TJ, but it was no use. He was at least twice my size and ten times stronger than me. As loud as I could, I yelled, "Lou, please let him go. It didn't mean anything. He is only a friend."

Lou released him and focused his thoughts on my words. Just as he turned my way, TJ took off like a rocket down the alley. My only guess was that it was a primal instinct for him to take off after living on the streets for so long. At that moment, all I wanted to do was punch Lou in the face for going off the way he did on TJ.

"What the hell were you thinking, Emma?" Lou demanded as his hands come up and wrapped around my upper arms.

"What the hell were you doing? You had no right going after him that way. He did nothing wrong," I hissed, pulling my body away from his grasp.

As I stepped back. I could feel my stomach begin to churn like something had taken up residence and was attempting to make its way out. Without warning, I found myself bent over, emptying the contents of my stomach on the black asphalt. Maybe this was what I deserved. I had certainly made a mess of everything. TJ was probably out of my life for good and Lou would never forgive me for what I did.

CHAPTER NINE
Gainer

I could feel my body begin to overheat the minute I saw that guy move in on Emma. I knew that she had at least four shots while I was there, and who knew how many she had before that. But when that guy placed his mouth over hers, I knew that things were just about to go from bad to very bad for her if I didn't do something. Even though I had done my own share of taking advantage of women while they were plastered, someone trying to take advantage of Emma hit home, and I just couldn't sit back and watch that happen.

Downing the rest of my Crown, I headed to the dance floor, needing to put an end to this. Pushing through the crowd of people, my hands began to tighten into fists and I could feel my body begin to tense. When I finally got to the lowlife who had his grubby hands on Emma, it took everything I had not to flatten his ass to the floor right there. Grabbing him by the shirt collar, the only thing I could think about was getting this guy outside and teaching him how to respect a woman. Even though Emma and I weren't officially together, I wasn't about to let any man touch her.

I could hear Emma yelling at me as I made my way to the back of the bar, but it didn't stop me from doing what needed to be done. Pushing the door open, my hand was still cinched to his collar. Positioning his body so that he was facing me, I cocked my hand back ready to lay into him when Emma's voice cried out.

As I listened to her explanation, I couldn't believe that she actually liked this guy. I could tell when she pushed me away that she was beyond pissed. Her arms came up between us as she pulled away from me. Before I could reach out to grab her, she was hurling her lunch.

"Emma, what the hell?" I asked, concerned as she looked up at me.

"I don't feel so well," she said, her face turning different shades of green.

Before she could protest, I had her up in my arms, walking in the direction of my truck. Given how sick she just got, I knew that she was going to be feeling pretty shitty in a couple of hours. Pulling open the passenger side door, I lifted her up onto the seat and made she was securely buckled in. By the time I got to my side of the truck and behind the wheel, Emma was out. If I had to guess, this was probably the first time she had ever drank. The way she was downing the shots, it made me think she had no idea what alcohol would do to her if she consumed so much in a short amount of time.

Looking over to Emma to make sure she was okay, she looked so helpless as her head kept bobbing back and forth. It was only then that I realized how beautiful she actually was. The dress she was wearing, although very sexy, was something that I could never imagine her wearing. She had a natural beauty about herself and the makeup she wore only enhanced her beauty more. Even though most of her lipstick was smeared on the outside of her lips, she was still the most gorgeous woman I had ever met.

Arriving at my apartment building, I pulled into my designated spot and turned off the engine. Emma was still out cold. Unable to take my eyes off her, I noticed that her dress had slid higher up her leg, revealing the soft creamy skin of her thigh. A man would have to be dead to not want to take her at that very moment. Shaking away my desires, I focused my thoughts on getting her up to my place and settled in. It was late enough in the evening that nobody was around when I got to the elevator. When I pushed the up button, Emma began stirring in my arms and I had to shift her in order to make sure I held her close.

As I watched the floors increase on the LED panel, all I could think about was how good it felt to be holding Emma in my arms. It was as though she was meant to be here, her body close to mine, just like this. The doors to the elevator opened and I once again shifted her to make sure she remained in my arms as I fumbled for the keys to my apartment. Once inside, I flipped on the dimmer light and proceeded to take her to my room, where I knew she would be the most comfortable. Placing her carefully on the bed, I held her upright as I began to lift her dress up over her head. I had no idea that the only article of clothing that she was wearing under the dress were her lacy panties. Removing her heeled shoes, I swung her legs onto the bed and pulled the comforter over her body. Emma gave a little moan before she finally settled. I could have stood beside the bed all night and just watched her as she slept, but lying beside her was a much better option or me.

Taking off all of my clothes except my boxers, I crawled under the covers beside her and pulled her body close to mine. Emma's body began to mold to mine as I slipped my arm around her. I wasn't much of a snuggler, but with Emma that all changed. Soon her cherry vanilla scent filled my mind and my eyes closed.

~****~

It seemed as though I had just closed my eyes as the sun began shining through the half-open vertical blinds of my floor-to-ceiling windows. Once again, my past crept inside my mind. Rolling over to my side, I looked over to the other side of the bed to find that Emma was still sound asleep. Careful not to wake her, I slipped from the bed and put my jeans on while heading out the door. I knew the minute she woke up, she was going to need some coffee, but more importantly, she would need a couple of aspirin to take care of the headache she was going to wake up to.

After finishing preparing the coffee, I headed to the front to get the daily paper that would be waiting for me on the other side. Opening the door, I picked it up and noticed the headline **"Unidentified woman found dead at Surge Nightclub."** I couldn't believe what I was reading. I was just there less than six hours ago. Placing the paper on the kitchen counter, I got a cup of coffee for myself and one for Emma. Heading back to the bedroom, I placed her cup of coffee on the nightstand and went into the bathroom to grab her some aspirin. I didn't think I was gone that long, but when I returned to the bedroom, she was no longer in the bed. Looking to the nightstand, I noticed that the coffee I had left her was gone. Knowing her all too well, I hurried out of the room to catch her before she left.

The minute I rounded the corner, I could hear her cry of desperation, "NO! Oh, God, no!"

"Emma, baby. What is it?" I asked, concerned.

When she turned around and was holding the newspaper, I knew exactly what had upset her. Her eyes were filled with tears as she focused on the front page. "Who would do this, Lou?" she asked frantically.

"Emma, do you know that girl?" I questioned.

"Yeah. She is one of the maids that worked at the Park Lane Hotel. Her name was Melissa," she replied, still holding the paper with a death grip.

Walking to her side, I removed the paper from her clutch and helped her to the couch. As we both sat, I began reading the article about the dead girl. Seems that they found her in the alley behind the nightclub. Someone had slit her throat. It went on to say that the officials didn't believe it was a mugging since her purse still contained all of her personal effects. They estimated that her time of death was around 1:30 a.m., which was only half an hour after we left. This could have been Emma.

Pulling her close to me, I could feel the warmth of her tears hit my chest. Stroking her soft hair, I could only think, *"What if it had been Emma lying in that alley?"* There had to be a reason that this girl died so heinously. Certainly, an autopsy would be performed and the medical examiner would be able to find out if there was any other foul play, and maybe even find some answers as to why this happened to her.

Kissing Emma on the forehead, I said softly, "Why don't you take a shower?"

"What are you going to do?" she asked with worry in her eyes.

"I'm not going anywhere, Emma. I'm going to get in touch with Peter and see if he can find out anything about this girl. Maybe we can find out why this happened and who did this."

"Peter?" she questioned.

"Yeah. He's the head of Jagged Edge Security."

"Maybe a shower would help," she replied, pushing from the couch with the white sheet she had taken from the bed wrapped around her body.

Waiting until she was out of earshot, I dialed Peter's number and waited for him to answer. I knew that he would be able to find out what happened to Emma's friend. He had friends at the NYPD that would be able to give him information.

Hearing his signature greeting, I said, "Peter, I need a favor."

"What's up, bro?" he asked.

After I told him what happened at Surge Nightclub, he offered to get in touch with his friend and let me know what he was able to find out. Placing my phone in my pocket, I headed to my bedroom to check on Emma. She was pretty upset about what had happened to her friend and I needed to make sure she was okay.

As I opened the door, I could hear the water running in the shower. Peeking my head inside, I could see just enough of Emma's body through the steamed glass of the shower to make my cock pulsate with need. Every curve of her body was perfect, and the way the soapy water ran down it made me hard just watching her. As much as I could have watched her longer, I knew that she would be finishing soon, and the last thing I needed was to be caught watching her.

As I was carefully closing the door so she wouldn't hear, my cell began to vibrate in my pocket. Looking down at the screen, it was Peter. "That was quick," I said, making my way back to the kitchen.

"Not so fast, bro. That's not why I'm calling." Peter paused for a moment before he continued. "There have been some developments on that guy who was killed at the Park Lane Hotel."

"What kind of developments?" I asked, curious to find out what was going on.

"The dead guy at the hotel has been identified as one Mr. Walsh McGowan."

"Seems as though I've heard that name before," I replied, trying to figure out where I knew the name.

"He was well known among the Catholic community. Who knows how many millions of dollars he has contributed to the Catholic orphanages? He has helped so many young people get a fresh start in life," Peter began, "I just don't understand what he was doing at the Park Lane Hotel and why the hell he was in possession of counterfeit money?"

As soon as Peter mentioned Catholic community and orphanage, my memory came back. I knew exactly who this man was. Help young people get a fresh start in life, my ass. I wish I could tell Peter the real truth about this man, but in doing so, I would have to reveal my past and I just wasn't ready to do that. My past was just that, and I wanted to keep it there as long as possible.

Hanging up with Peter, I didn't realize I had been daydreaming until I heard Emma's voice behind me. "Who were you talking to?"

"It was Peter. I thought he could get in touch with his contact at the NYPD to find out why your friend was killed," I replied stepping closer to where she was. Even though she seemed to be feeling better, I could tell that she was still shaken up about the death of her friend Melissa. Pulling her near me, I whispered, "How about we get out of here? I'll take you home and you can change. We can spend the day not worrying about anything."

I knew that was going to be tough for her, but if I could get her mind off of what happened, maybe then I could get to know her better. Slowly, I was making headway, and I felt like she was beginning to trust me.

CHAPTER TEN
Emma

I thought I was living a nightmare when I saw Melissa's picture on the front page of the newspaper. It had reminded me so much of my mom, when they had placed that white sheet over her body thinking she was dead as the blood pooled around her head. I will never forget that day as long as I live. It was my first day at the hotel, and after getting off, I walked through Central Park, taking a shortcut to where my mom and the rest of the homeless people stayed. There was so much commotion going on by the bridge to Belvedere Castle, and as I walked down the trail, my curiosity got the best of me. It was late, and if it hadn't it been for the lighting in the park, I wouldn't have been able to see what was going on. Then I saw the white sheet. I had no idea who was under it, but when the police officer lifted the sheet to show another officer the body, I knew then that it was my mom. I had never felt so helpless in my life.

When I walked up to her body, the police officer tried to keep me away from her, but when I yelled out that it was my mom, he let me go. Kneeling beside her, I could feel the coldness of her blood beneath my knees. I had never prayed so much in my life, but as I did, there was movement under the sheet. First it was her hand reaching out to me. Pulling back the sheet, her eyes fluttered open. It was only for a second, but it was long enough to let me know that my prayers had been answered. I had never yelled so loud in my life.

I never knew exactly what happened to her that day, but the doctor said she had so much heroin in her body that it was a wonder she didn't die. He also said that may have been what saved her life. Whoever split her head open must have thought she was dead. Sometimes I think that she would have been better off. Now she doesn't even know she has a daughter, let alone her name.

~****~

"You are awfully quiet, baby. What's on your mind?" Lou asked as we headed towards the motel.

"I was just thinking about Melissa. Who would do this to her?" I frowned, feeling a tight knot in my stomach.

"I don't know, Emma, but we are going to find out."

Lou took hold of my hand and squeezed it gently before bringing it to his lips and placing a soft kiss on it. It was comforting to know that he cared and was willing to find out what happened to Melissa. Letting go of my hand, Lou made a quick turn, which brought us to the parking lot of the motel. When he pulled into a parking spot and turned off the engine, I muttered, "I will only be a minute. No need for you to come up."

Opening the door to his truck, I got out and walked the short distance to the concrete steps. One at a time, I climbed them, feeling completely numb. Reaching my room, I went inside and was reminded of last night by all of the items I left scattered on the bathroom counter as I got ready. Shoving everything inside the trash can, I fell to the bed, letting my feelings get the best of me. Hearing a light knock on the door, I wiped the tears from my face and pushed myself from the bed. When I opened the door, Lou was standing on the other side. It was like he knew exactly how I was feeling. His arms wrapped around me, bringing my body close to his.

Holding me at arm's length, he brushed a stray hair from my face and lowered his head until our lips met. Consumed by his warmth, I was helpless as I pushed to my tiptoes to meet his demand as he parted my lips. The mere touch of his mouth to mine sent a shock wave through my body, leaving my head spinning. Breaking our connection, his eyes fell upon mine and I could only feel the beating of my heart as he said, "No one will ever want you as much as I do."

I wasn't sure what he meant, but at that very moment, he was the only man that I ever wanted as well. Wrapping my arms tighter around his shoulders, I pulled him closer as I pressed my mouth to his. Without warning, my body was off of the floor and cradled against his body. Lou walked us to the bed, where he gently lowered me. It didn't matter that my clothes and things were scattered across it. All that mattered was that I needed him. With our lips glued together, I began tugging at his t-shirt like a mad woman. The only way I was going to be able to get it off him was to break our connection. No sooner than his shirt was off, our lips once again found each other. Taking hold of my arms, Lou placed them above my head and held them in place with one strong hand. Keeping me from moving (but more than anything I didn't want to), Lou trailed his other hand down the soft material of my dress to where my thigh was exposed. Slipping his hand between my skin and my dress, he caressed my sensitized skin as he worked his hand up my dress. Pushing my dress further up my body, I could feel the warmth of his hand as he lowered it underneath my panties. More than anything, I wanted this. When he released my hands, I pulled him to me as I struggled to undo the zipper on his jeans.

Even though our bodies were so close together, I managed to get his zipper down before he kneeled before me and worked my dress the rest of the way up my body. With my dress off, he rose from the bed, reached into his pocket, and pulled out a small packet before taking his jeans off. Sitting beside me, he looked down at my nakedness and stated softly, "I want you, Emma, but only if you want this."

I wanted this more than anything. Taking a breath, I gazed into his eyes and said with conviction, "I want this more than I have ever wanted anything in my life."

Lou lowered his head and placed his mouth over mine, letting me know that he wouldn't hurt me. My mind was reeling with pleasure as the velvet warmth of his kiss continued down my neck to the valley of my breasts before he tenderly fondled one small peak with his tongue. As he continued to tease my taut pink nipple, I could feel the moisture begin to pool between my legs. Not only was I wet with desire, but my heart was beating so fast, I thought it was going to come right out of my chest.

Moving further down my body, I could feel the warmth of his mouth as he trailed soft kisses over the plane of my sensitized skin. While one hand was still caressing my taut nipple, the other began exploring the apex of my sex. I knew soon he would feel just what his touch was doing to me. When his hand fell between my legs, I spread them wider, allowing him the access he needed. With a gentle push, he worked his finger inside my channel. The back and forth movement caused my hips to push against him as he plunged it deeper and deeper inside. Never had I felt something so wonderful. It was like dying and going to heaven. His assault was soon halted as I watched him wrap his hand around his cock and stroke it gently. It was the sexiest thing I had ever seen. Just as he stroked it, his erection grew and my heart began beating faster. Taking the small packet between his teeth, he tore it open and removed the latex condom. Never had I seen a man sheath himself. Now more than ever I wanted him.

"I am going to go really slow, baby. The minute it gets to be too much, I will stop until you tell me to continue." Lou met my eyes before placing a soft kiss on my lips.

Nodding my head, I closed my eyes and began feeling every movement, waiting in anticipation for the pleasure he was going to give me. Placing his cock at my entrance, I could feel my walls begin to stretch to accommodate his size. Lou's movements were slow and gentle as he inched his way inside. The feeling of fullness struck with a slight discomfort. I could feel my body tense and my grip tightened on Lou's shoulders as he continued his drive inside me. Then it hit. Pleasure mixed with pain consumed me. It was unlike anything I would ever be able to describe. As quickly as it came, it was gone, and only complete bliss remained.

Rocking my hips to mimic Lou's movements, I could feel my body relax and take him completely. Every thrust made me want more. Changing his position, Lou lifted my hips from the bed and cupped my ass as he continued to push deeper inside me. The sensation of our bodies moving together took over and my body let go with thunder. What he did to me had me reeling. I was so overtaken by the pleasure that my emotions soon took over and the tears of contentment spilled.

"Baby, are you okay? Did I hurt you?" his voice beckoned as he gazed down on me.

"No. It's just that… you just gave me something that I will never forget. Thank you."

~****~

Lou and I laid in bed for what seemed like only minutes, but was actually hours, before we decided to shower. Even though the motel shower was nowhere near the magnificence of his, we were still able to take one together. It seemed like a good idea at the time, but by the time we had finished exploring each other further, the hot water had turned to cold. I would have thought that a motel of this size would at least be able to provide enough water for a long shower.

Once we were dried off, Lou suggested that we have a picnic in the park. He knew of a good deli that prepared the best sandwiches ever, and with a bottle of sparkling wine, we would have the perfect lunch. I had spent a lot of time in the park over the years, but to actually have a picnic and just sit and enjoy it was something that I had never done. Most of the time I wandered along the paths looking through the trash cans for something worth eating, which wouldn't make me sick.

Slipping on my tennis shoes, I grabbed my bag, which held a blanket from the motel, and followed Lou to his truck. Just as we reached the bottom of the steps, I caught sight of TJ, who seemed to be purposely staying out of sight, behind the tree a few yards away from the building.

Handing Lou my bag, I said, "Give me a few minutes."

"I don't think it is wise for you to be talking to that guy. He nearly had sex with you last night on the dance floor," Lou cursed.

"Lou, he's a friend. I will only be a minute," I replied, seeing Lou's frustration as he raked his fingers through his blonde hair.

As soon as Lou was far enough away, I walked over to TJ to find out what he was doing at the motel. The closer I got to him, the more I could see that something was off about him. The way he looked wasn't new to me. I faced it every day with my mom. Standing a safe distance from him, I asked cautiously, "What are you doing here, TJ?"

"I came to see you," he answered, coming a little closer.

Looking him over from head to toe, he was definitely on something, "Are you high, TJ?"

"Maybe, maybe not. What does it matter?" he grinned.

"I think it would be better if you left."

As I turned to head back to the truck, TJ grabbed my arm and pulled my body to his. Without warning his mouth was over mine, forcing his tongue between my lips. I tried to push him away, but he was too strong. Turning my face away from him, I could see Lou running double time up the parking lot. TJ's arm that was wrapped around my waist eased as Lou bent his fingers back, causing him to let go of me. As soon as I moved out of the way, Lou had TJ in a choke hold.

"You should have listened to me the first time, asshole," Lou cursed as he tightened his grip around TJ's neck.

As much as I wanted Lou to hurt TJ, I didn't want him to kill him. In a loud tone, I yelled to Lou, "Let him go, Lou. He is high on something."

"Him being high is no excuse for what he did," Lou hissed.

"Please, Lou, let him go."

"You're lucky that Emma is here to prevent me from hurting you. This is your final warning. STAY AWAY FROM HER!" Lou advised between gritted teeth.

"Okay, okay," TJ mumbled, looking straight at me.

Lou loosened the hold he had on TJ. When TJ was free, he turned towards Lou and glared at him. It was almost like he was in a trance. Shaking his head, he began to walk away. Lou turn to him and scratched his head as though he was confused about something.

Walking up behind him. I grabbed his arm and said, "Thank you for not hurting him."

"Yeah, well, next time he might not be so lucky. There is something about that guy that seems familiar. Like I know him from somewhere. How do you know him, anyway?" Lou asked.

"He is just a friend," I countered, giving Lou the least amount of information as possible, but still answering his question.

"That really doesn't tell me anything. Where did you two meet?" Lou persisted.

I wasn't sure what to say. I certainly couldn't tell him the truth, so I lied. "We went to school together."

My answer must have satisfied him, because he didn't ask me any more about TJ as we drove to the park. Heading to the north entrance of Central Park, I kept thinking about what would cause TJ to use drugs. Looking back to when I first met him by the bridge, I knew that he wasn't using drugs then, but seeing him now, something had changed for him. Even though he came at me the way that he did, I still wanted him to be my friend, Hopefully, he wouldn't be taking Lou's advice and stay away from me. I really needed to know what his deal was.

CHAPTER ELEVEN
Gainer

As much as I wanted to flatten that guy, I knew that if I wanted any kind of relationship with Emma, I had to ease up on him. I spent the entire time at the park trying to figure out where I might have met the guy. It was driving me crazy and Emma was beginning to notice my preoccupation with this guy.

"If you know him, Lou, it will come to you. In the meantime, let's go watch the little kids sail their motorized boats on Conservatory Water," Emma suggested.

I knew that Emma was right. The last thing that I needed was to rack my brain about where I knew that dude from. Gathering our things, I placed them inside Emma's bag and slung it over my shoulder. Just like every other Saturday, the Park was packed with people taking advantage of the nice weather. Even the dogs were having a heyday as they were thrown Frisbees to catch by their respectable owners. There were also a lot of kids fishing, hoping to catch the big one.

When we finally made to the Conservatory Water, we found an empty bench where we could sit and watch the RC sailboats being expertly maneuvered through the smooth-as-glass water. Taking Emma's hand and placing a soft kiss on it, I watched her enjoy the many boats on the water.

"When I was a little girl, me and my mom used to spend hours watching the little boats glide through the water," she confessed.

"You never mention her. Is she still living?" I asked, wanting to learn everything about her.

"It's complicated," she said.

"You can tell me anything, Emma." I needed to let her know that no matter what, I was never going to change the way I felt about her.

Her eyes lowered to her lap as she began explaining her circumstances. "My mom doesn't live in New York. She lives in an adult care facility in Illinois. She's been there for some time."

"I'm sorry, Emma. Do ever go to see her?" I asked.

"No. It is really expensive and I can't afford it."

"Maybe, someday, we can see her together." As soon as I offered to go with her, Emma's demeanor had changed. The look on her face told me that her mom being in a care facility was more than that.

The minute Emma stood and said, "We better go," I wished I could take back my offer.

Heading back to the truck, Emma seemed stand-offish. As much as I tried to find out more about her, the harder it was. Most of her answers were short and general, to the point that I quit talking and just walked with her. Nearing the truck, I took the bag from her and set it on the back seat. Opening her door, I waited until she was settled before closing it.

On the way to her motel, the ride was becoming excruciatingly painful with nothing but silence between us.

Taking hold of her hand, I tried to get her attention, but her focus was on the street I was driving on. Unable to stand it anymore, I finally broke. "Emma, did I say something to offend you?"

With her eyes drawn to mine, she replied in a low, soft voice, "No."

Again with the one-word answers, I responded, "Then why the sudden silence?"

Pulling her hand from my grasp, she folded them on her lap before looking out the windshield. "There are some things that you don't know about me, and right now, I'm afraid if I told you, you would disappear."

"I would never do that, Emma. I really like you and anything you have to say is not going to change the way I feel about you." No one's life could be more fucked up than mine, so whatever it was she was keeping from me couldn't begin to compare to what I was keeping from her.

"My mom didn't just end up in the nursing home because she got sick. She was addicted to heroin and someone beat the shit out of her. Even the doctor was surprised she survived the beating. He credited it to the amount of drugs that were in her system. Now she can't even remember her own daughter," she confessed with a strained voice.

It pained me to see her so sad. It had to be very hard for her being in New York with her mom so far away. Pulling over to the side of the street, I put the truck into park and placed my hand in hers. If it hadn't been for the center console, I would have had her in my lap. As she looked to me, a lonely tear began to fall down her cheek. With my index finger, I wiped it away and watched as she kept her eyes to mine. Moving in closer to her, I tilted my head until our lips met. As I kissed her, I could taste the hint of salt on her soft lips from the tears that she had shed earlier.

Breaking our kiss, I cupped her cheek with my hand and blurted, "I want to do something for you. Let me take you to see your mom. Maybe if she saw you, she would remember you."

"You would do that for me," she sighed.

"I would do anything for you, Emma."

The fact of the matter was that I was beginning to fall for her and I would cross the Sahara Desert if it meant she would be happy. Giving her one last kiss, I put the truck into drive and pulled away from the curb. Trying to keep my eyes on where I was going, I couldn't help but look over to Emma to see that her tears had finally stopped falling. Not only that, but I could have sworn there was even a hint of a smile on her face.

When we got to her motel, I grabbed the bag from the back seat and rounded the car and waited for Emma to get out. As we came closer to her room, I could tell that something was wrong. The door to her room was cracked open and I knew that when we left, it was closed. Grabbing her arm, I whispered as I pulled her back, "Stay here."

I could see that she was ready to argue, but her mouth clamped shut the minute I nodded my head in a 'no' motion. When I knew she understood, I dropped the bag on the concrete and headed slowly towards her room. It was at that moment that I wished I had my gun. I only hoped that if there was still someone inside, they wouldn't be armed. Standing just to the right of the door, I placed my hand on the cool metal and began slowly pushing it open. Looking between the small crack by the door hinges, I searched for any movement. When there wasn't any, I continued to push the door further open.

Confident that whomever had broken inside her room was gone, I entered the room to find that the room was just as we left it. Stepping outside the door. I motioned to Emma that it was safe to come inside. As she stepped past me, she said with a puzzled look, "Maybe we forgot to close the door when we left."

"Emma, the door was closed. Do you see anything missing?" I asked, looking around the room myself.

Emma began looking around, studying the room to see if she could find anything gone. When she let out a loud gasp, I knew something was wrong. "What is it, Emma?"

She didn't say a word. All she could do was point towards the cupboard. I had to get behind her to see what she was pointing at. The hidden safe in the cabinet was opened. By her reaction, I knew that there must have been something of importance inside the safe that was now gone. Placing my hands on her arms, I positioned her body towards mine and asked, "What was in the safe, baby?"

As I held on to her, I could feel her body tremble. Whatever she kept safely tucked away in that safe had to have meant a lot to her. Lifting her chin so that I could see her face. I realized then that she was fuming. Her trembling wasn't because she was upset, it was because she was pissed. "My whole future was in that safe," she asserted, lifting her hands to her face. "Now I have nothing. I am back where I was before."

"What was in the safe, Emma, that could change your life?" I asked, confused by her confession. "Nothing could be that important."

"Yeah, well, I'm sure you have never been without in your life."

If only she knew what a shit life I had. It was then that I decided to come clean with her. Maybe if I confessed, she would open up to me. Taking her by the hand, I led her to the bed and waited for her to take a seat before taking my place beside her. Clearing my mind, I took in a deep breath and began telling her about my past. "Not everyone has a perfect life, Emma. My life was far from perfect. I don't even know who my mother was. I was raised in a Catholic orphanage from the time I was a baby until I left to join the military. Things that happened in that orphanage would make your stomach turn. I was never so happy as when the day came that I could finally leave that place."

Turning my way, I thought for sure Emma was going to finally open up to me, but instead she asked softly, "What kinds of things, Lou?"

"Things that shouldn't happen to little boys." Leaving it at that, I stood and held out my hand to Emma, "Come on, let's get out of here."

Even though it wasn't my day to teach my martial arts class, I thought it would be nice to go to the YMCA and show Emma another part of my life. Maybe she would even allow me to show her a few moves.

Making certain that the door was closed and secured, we both headed down to where I had parked the truck. Once inside I drove down Central Park West. The YMCA was a short distance from her motel and it would only take a few minutes to get there. As we were driving, I could hear what sounded like the theme from 'Rocky' start playing. Emma reached inside her pocket and pulled out her phone. Trying to concentrate on the road, I listened intently to the conversation.

"What?" she said, holding her phone tightly to her ear so that the voice on the other end couldn't be heard.

As her conversation continued, I could tell by the tone in her voice that she was really pissed at the person on the other end. With her final words, "Screw you," I knew that the person on the other end just got humbled and she wasn't about to put up with any shit.

Curious as to whom she could have been talking to, I demanded, "Who the hell was that, Emma?"

"Work," she snapped.

"Sounded pretty intense," I remarked, pretty confident that it was someone other than work.

"Yeah, well, that's what happens when you mess up," she replied.

Holding back what I wanted to say, I pulled up in front of the YMCA and put the truck into park. Emma had the door open before I could say anything. By the time I got out, she was up the stairs and heading inside. Her taking off like that, half-cocked, was about to end. Running up the steps, I caught her just in time to grab her by the hand. Her head swung around so fast, I thought for sure she was going to dislocate it. "Why are you always trying to get away from me?" I questioned, demanding and answer.

"I'm not running away. I just don't like the feeling of being judged or disbelieved."

"I never said that I didn't believe you, Emma," I argued.

"Maybe not in so many words, but I wasn't born yesterday, it's written all over your face."

Maybe I did have a hard believing that it was work calling, but in no way did I mean to judge her. All I wanted was for her to let me in and tell me what was really going on. Squeezing her hand tighter, I pulled her close to me and lowered my mouth to hers. At first, she hesitated in returning the kiss, but then her lips parted to let me in. Between the heat of our kiss, I said the only thing I could. "I'm sorry."

CHAPTER TWELVE
Emma

I could have thrown my phone out the window. When TJ called, I thought for sure that he was calling to apologize for the way he acted earlier. I had no idea it was to tell me that it was him that took the money from the safe in my room. I didn't even have to ask him how he got in my room or how he was able to get into the safe. I guess he knew me pretty well. I should have never used the digits of my birthday as the code, zero-nine-one-seven. It wasn't too hard for him to figure it out, since he was still living under the bridge and helped celebrate my birthday. My present from him was a Snickers candy bar with a single candle placed in the middle.

Lou always managed to make things better, though; as angry as I was at him for not believing what I said, his kiss took all of that away. When his lips met mine, it was like I was in a different place and time. It was only us, no sadness, only rainbows and butterflies filled the space. The feeling didn't last long though. Two spectators brought us back to the here and now when their little giggles filled the air. Breaking our kiss, Lou looked over to the two young boys and said, "Now that is how you kiss a woman."

I had never seen that shade of red on any one person. Lou opened the door and the two boys hurried up the steps, making their escape inside the building. Heading in ourselves, the sound of voices filled the air as we walked down the wide hallway to the gym area. I was surprised to see so many young people inside the building; most of them were boys playing basketball on half of the court. The other half of the court was set up for anyone who wanted to hit a few balls over the net. As we walked to the other side of the court, most of the boys recognized Lou by waving to him and saying, "Hi."

Looking over to the boys, I said with a smile. "Your fan club, I presume."

"I guess you could call it that," he replied.

Once past the gym court, Lou and I went through a metal door, which brought us to another hallway. Turning to the right, we came upon another door, which Lou stopped at.

Pulling a set of keys from his pocket, he unlocked the door and pulled it open. It was dark when we went through the door, but not for long, Lou flipped the light switch on and I could that it was another gym, only much smaller, with mats covering the majority of the floor.

A little bit confused, I entered. I scanned the room and asked, "Any particular reason why we are here?"

"I thought maybe you would want to learn some of what I teach my students," he said.

"Students?" I asked, totally confused.

"Yeah, I teach martial arts to some of the kids. Three times a week," he added.

"So, you think you can teach me a thing or two about martial arts?"

"I would sure like to try."

Lou had a smile on his face that could have convinced me to do anything he asked. Leading me to the middle of the room, he began showing me a breathing exercise that was supposed to help in clearing my mind. As I breathed in and out, I had to admit that it was working. My body felt relaxed. All of the tension was gone and I began feeling my mind clear.

After we had finished out breathing exercise, Lou began showing me different positions. It almost felt like I was in the movie *Karate Kid*. *"Wax on, wax off."* I couldn't help but start laughing. I was laughing so hard that I fell to the floor holding my side, because I couldn't stop. When the door to the gym opened and a teenage kid walked in, my laughing spell eased as he approached Lou.

Putting his hands together, he bowed to Lou like he was someone important and said, "Hello, Sensei."

"What the heck is a Sensei?" I asked as I watched Lou return the bow.

Turning to me, he held out his hand to help me up and replied with a smile, "Teacher."

Lou walked over to the young man and whispered something in his ear. As I stood on the mat, without warning, they began going after each other. I was just about ready to yell at them to stop when it dawned on me that they were only putting on a show. I couldn't believe how much precision each move had. It was almost like they were dancing with one another, but on a fighting level. Neither one of them outdid the other. When they had finally finished the demonstration, Lou walked over to me and said, "This is what I teach. Someday I would like to teach you the art of karate."

I was at a loss for words. I would never be able to do what they just did, but I also knew that Lou would never take no for an answer. While I stood thinking about what he said, Lou walked the young man to the door. Thinking that he was far enough away, he dug into his back pocket and pulled out his wallet. I was pretty sure that Lou gave the boy a couple of twenties. It was the sweetest thing I had ever seen, but I also knew that it was something I needed to keep to myself, at least for now.

~****~

Waking up feeling the soreness of muscles that I didn't even know I had, I tried to ease my body out of bed. I loved spending the day with Lou at the YMCA. There was a side of him that I really liked. Not only was he a great teacher, he really cared about the kids that went there. It made me wonder how many there actually were.

Barely able to make it to the bathroom, I turned on the water to the shower and slowly began removing my clothes. As I looked in the mirror, I couldn't believe how bruised my upper arms were, and my upper legs. Lou was really gentle with me as he showed me the different defense moves, so I knew that they couldn't have come from him. They had to have been from landing on the mat after falling several times when trying to land my punches or kicks. One thing about it, they looked a lot worse than they felt.

When I was finally able to lift my leg high enough to step inside the tub, the water on my sore muscles felt like heaven. I could have stayed like this all day, but I knew that eventually the hot water would be gone and I would end up freezing my ass off. Until then, I was going to use every drop of hot water there was.

Standing under the stream of hot water, I started thinking about the money that TJ took and what I was going to do. I only had a few more days left before I would have to leave the motel and go back to living on the streets. The only idea that came to mind was convincing TJ that there was enough money for both of us to share. Surely he would be willing to share. I thought about threatening him with going to the cops, but then that would lead to an investigation, which would lead to more problems for me, and I just couldn't do that.

Ending my shower and getting dressed. I unplugged my cell from its charger and found TJ's contact number and waited for him to answer.

"I was wondering when you were going to call me back," he stated.

"All I want to know is why. Why did you take my money?" I demanded.

"Oh, come on, Emma. You think I would be stupid enough to believe that the money was actually yours?" he replied with a chuckle.

"Mine or not, you had no right to take it. I want it back, or at least half of it."

"No can do, babe. The money is gone."

"What do you mean, gone?" My heart was racing. If he spent all that money he had better hope that I never saw him again because if I did, I was going to kill him.

"Your little stash helped me to pay off a debt that was long overdue. You might have just saved my life. Gotta go."

"Wait..." The phone went dead before I got the chance to ask where. Ringing TJ again, it went right to voicemail, which told me that he must have turned his phone off.

I couldn't believe that this was happening to me. Slumping on the bed, I began rubbing my head to try and figure out what I was going to do. I didn't have much time before I would be out on the street again. Grabbing my small purse. I opened it up to see how much money I had left. By the time I finished counting it, there was only one hundred twenty dollars. This was not enough money for what I needed. Stuffing it back inside my small purse, I leaned back on the bed and just stared at the ceiling. Knowing that there had to be another way to get off the street, I pulled myself together and stopped feeling sorry for myself. Thinking that I would just need to find another job, I took a couple of dollars from my purse and decide to go to the motel office and grab a paper.

The minute I opened the door, a gentleman in a suit and a woman in slacks and a silky blouse appeared in front of me. "Ms. Atwood?" the man asked.

"Yes, I'm she," I answered hesitantly.

"My name is Detective Shaw and this is Detective Bentley. We have a few questions for you."

I had no idea what the cops would be doing here or how they even found me. The only thought that was running through my mind was the money. They must have found out that I took it. Moving to the side, I allowed them to enter my room. Closing the door, Detective Shaw had his cell phone in his hand, searching for something. Holding it out to me, he showed me a picture of Kate, one of the girls from the Park Lane Hotel.

"Do you know this girl, Ms. Atwood?" the woman detective asked.

"Yeah, she works at the Park Lane. She's a maid." I replied, looking up at Detective Shaw, confused.

"She was found dead this morning in her apartment. Her throat was slit," he divulged.

It was like I had run into a brick wall. My legs gave out and I fell down on the bed. I couldn't believe what I had just heard. Two girls that I knew were dead, and they both worked at the hotel.

"Ms. Atwood, are you okay? You don't look so well," Shaw pointed out before continuing. "Do you know of any reason why someone would want to kill her?"

"Are you kidding me? How the hell would I know?"

"Well, if you hear of anything, please let us know." Detective Shaw handed me his card as I just sat there in shock.

As soon as they left, I pulled my phone from my pocket and dialed Lou. I heard his voice on the second ring.

"Lou, I need your help. I think I'm in trouble."

CHAPTER THIRTEEN
Gainer

Finishing my workout, I was surprised to see Emma's number appear on the screen. What surprised me even more was the sound of her voice. I could tell that she was upset, and when she said she was in trouble, it didn't take me long to grab my keys and head over to the motel where she was staying. Heading down to the parking garage, everything bad that I could think about entered my mind. Even the drive to the motel was filled with concern for her.

Putting my truck into park, I headed up the steps to Emma's room. When she opened the door, I could tell that she had been crying. I wasn't even inside before she wrapped her arms around me and said, "Lou, I'm so scared."

Comforting her the best I could, I held her tight to my body and asked, "What's going on, baby?"

"It's Kate, they found her dead in her apartment. Her throat was slit just like Melissa's," she blurted in a trembling voice.

"Who is Kate, Emma?" I asked, confused by what she just told me.

"She works at the hotel. She was one of the girls that went out with us to Surge. Now she's dead. What if I am next, Lou?"

As I held her tightly in my arms, the tears from her eyes began to spill. All I knew was that if these two murders were connected, there was a good possibility that she *could* be next. I just needed to figure out what that connection was. One thing I knew for sure was she wasn't going to stay in this motel any longer. If I had any chance in protecting her, I needed to keep her close, and in order to do that she would need to stay with me.

"Emma, grab your things. You're staying with me for a while," I commanded gently.

"Lou, who could be doing this?" she asked in a small, childlike voice.

"I don't know, baby, but me and the guys are going to find out."

Kissing her lightly on the forehead, I watched as she gathered her things. I couldn't believe that everything she owned fit inside the one bag. The same bag she had protected when we first met. As she loaded the empty bag with her things, I noticed that she no longer had the cans of food that she was packing a few days ago. As she placed the last of her things inside the bag, I walked up to her and took hold of the strap, slinging it over my shoulder.

"You go check out. I'll meet you at the truck," I said.

Nodding her head, she followed me out of the door and down the concrete steps. While I went straight, she headed to the motel office to turn in her key and to take care of her bill. I didn't know what I was thinking. Hurrying to the truck, I set her bag on the back seat and sprinted to the office. The least I could do for her was to pay her bill. I knew that she didn't have much money, and even though this place couldn't have been much per night, I knew that it was going to make a big dent in her wallet to pay the bill.

Opening the door to the office, I saw that the manager was actually handing her money back. This was a first for me. I had never seen money be given back to a guest, unless of course their stay was paid in advance and they were refunded the days they weren't staying. He must have handed her at least three hundred dollars, if not more.

"Sorry you had to cut your stay short, Miss," the manager stated.

The door slammed so hard that it alerted Emma and the manager of my arrival. Stuffing the money in her pocket, she said good-bye to the manager and walked towards me. Pushing the door open for her, I handed her the keys and said, "I'll be just a minute."

When the door closed and Emma was on her way to the truck, I walked over to the manager and asked, "Can you tell me how long Emma has been staying here?"

"A good week and a half. She was a nice girl, paid for her stay in advance, nine hundred-sixty dollars to be exact," he confessed.

Trying to digest what he just said, I found it hard to believe that Emma would have that kind of money. "Thanks," I said as I headed out the door.

Emma was waiting in the truck, ready to go. Getting in, I looked over to her and asked, "Ready?"

~****~

It was going to be different, but in a good kind of way, to have Emma here with me while the guys and I figured out who was behind the deaths of her friends. I wasn't sure what Emma preferred as far as the sleeping arrangements, so I did the gentlemanly thing and placed her things in the guest bedroom. It was only after she picked up her bag and looked at me with those beautiful brown eyes that I knew what she really wanted.

Confirming what I already knew, she asked, "I'd like to stay with you in your room, if that's okay?"

"Of course, I would love for you to stay with me." How could I say no to her? Having her with me in my bed was like a dream come true.

After getting the sleeping arrangements sorted out, I decided to cook a nice wholesome meal for her. Even though Emma was the most gorgeous woman I had ever seen, it wouldn't hurt for her to put on a few pounds. While I prepared dinner, Emma sat at the breakfast bar watching me, inquiring about where I learned how to cook and what it was exactly that I was making.

One of the best things that I could have learned in the military was how to cook. I actually think all of the brothers at Jagged Edge were the best of the best when it came to cooking. As I stood by the stove sautéing the onions and mushrooms, Emma asked softly, "Can I help with anything?"

Turning towards her, I replied with a smile, "You can set the table if you want."

Once I showed her where the plates and silverware were, she walked over to the dining table and began setting the table, only it wasn't really setting it as she just placed the plates on the table with the silverware stacked on top. Trying hard to contain my amusement, I said, "Thank you."

"Where did this woman come from?" I thought to myself. There was no way that she could have been so

ignorant to the basic ways of life. Testing my theory, I asked her with a smile, "So, do you cook?"

"Are you kidding? I barely know how to open a can of beans, let alone cook a meal," she confessed.

"So, your mom never showed you how to cook?" I inquired.

"Mom was off doing her own thing. She never had time to show me how to cook."

"I guess you never sat down together and shared a good meal then?"

I must have overstepped my bounds, because Emma was up off her chair heading to the bedroom. Turning off the stove, I said, "Emma, wait."

Emma stopped where she was with her hands clenched into tight fists. Turning to face me, she placed her hands on her hips and sputtered, "I am not like you, Lou. I haven't been given things, for your information, and that includes proper dining etiquette. My mom did the best she could for me and whatever she couldn't give me, I did for myself."

"I didn't mean it that way, Emma," I backpedaled. I never thought that what I said would have been taken the wrong way. "I just meant that sitting down to a home-cooked meal might not have been something you did a lot of. That's all."

Moving towards her, I took her by the hand and pulled her close. The minute her eyes met mine, I couldn't help but lower my lips to hers. Even though she didn't move away from me, I could feel her hesitancy. Breaking our connection, I rubbed my finger across her lips and said, "I'm sorry if I hurt you."

With a slight nod, she replied, "I'm sorry I over-reacted."

Emma followed me back into the kitchen, where I turned the stove back on and finished cooking our meal. She took her place at the breakfast bar looking absolutely beautiful, as usual. Grabbing the pan of sautéed mushrooms, I placed it on the other burner and checked on chicken that I had baking in the oven. Pouring us each a glass of wine, I took our dinner to the table and separated the plates and silverware. Emma took her place next to me as I sat the head of the table.

The minute she took a bite, I could tell that she was impressed by my cooking talent. Hearing her moan with every bite was beginning to have an effect on my manhood. It was a good thing that I was seated at the table. When the time came for her to take the last bite, I couldn't be happier. The confinement in my jeans was causing a very uncomfortable strain on my cock.

Gathering a couple of dishes to hide the effect she was having on me, I headed to the sink to drop them off. Thankfully, Emma remained at the table while she finished drinking her glass of wine. This kind of thing never happened to me before, at least not in that manner.

Finishing the dishes, I suggested that we have another glass of wine and sit on the couch and relax. As we sat there, Emma's thoughts were a million miles away. I had called out her name several times, but she didn't hear me. Placing my hand on her leg, I said in a soft tone. "What is going on in that pretty little head of yours?"

Reverting her focus from the view out the window to me, she replied with a whimper, "I feel helpless with what happened to Melissa and Kate. I wish there was something that I could do to help find who did this to them." She took in a deep breath before continuing. "Even though I didn't know them that well, I would have loved to. I don't know very many people. It would have been nice to have them as friends.

Her head slowly fell to my shoulder and I felt the need to wrap my arm around her. I had a funny feeling just by the way she acted that she didn't have very many friends, and the one friend she did have was trouble in my book, and really not worth having as a friend. He was a lowlife scumbag and not a good person for Emma to know. There was still something about him. I knew I had seen him before. I just couldn't for the life of me remember where.

Taking a chance, I decide to see if Emma would be willing to give me some information on him. Kissing her lightly on the head, I came out with it. "You said that you knew TJ from school, have you two kept in touch all this time?"

"No. Not really. He came by the motel a few days ago wanting to catch up," she shared.

"So, what is old TJ up to nowadays?"

"He said something about working at one of those call centers. I guess he is a day shift manager there."

"Really. He doesn't seem like the manger type," I pointed out.

"Yeah, I'm beginning to think that too," Emma stated.

"Why is that, baby?" I questioned.

"Can we talk about something else besides TJ?" Emma requested, tilting her head upward.

"How about we just sit and enjoy the view?" I suggested.

Pulling Emma closer to my body, I took a sip of my wine and just sat looking out the window until darkness came. I loved Manhattan, especially at night. Who could ask for anything more than a beautiful woman in your arms and a beautiful view to go along with it?

CHAPTER FOURTEEN
Emma

The last thing I remembered was falling asleep on the couch in Lou's arms. But when I woke up the next morning in his bed, I had no argument, since I couldn't have been more comfortable with Lou's arms wrapped around my body. Turning my head slightly, I took in a breath, smelling his scent on my pillow. If there was a way that I could put it in a bottle and save for later, I would in a heartbeat.

Feeling his body move, I rolled over and watched as his eyes began to open. I was pretty sure the magnificent color in his gray eyes was because of the reflection of the sun shining through the blinds that were slightly drawn. Placing my hand on his cheek, I said softly. "I could stare at you for hours."

With a small chuckle, he smiled, "Only hours? Because I could look at you for days, maybe even years."

His words were the sweetest thing I had ever heard. I leaned in, meaning only to give him a short kiss, but his arms wrapped around my body and soon I was on my back with his strong sexy body hovering above me. Gently moving the hair that had fallen on my face, he whispered softly, "You are the most beautiful woman I have ever laid eyes on."

Without another word, his mouth was over mine and the warmth of his tongue slipped between my waiting lips. I may have been overly excited, but I pulled him even closer, deepening our kiss. I was mystified by my own desire for this man as the thought of what would happen next sent my head into a wild swirl. Frantically going at each other like we would disappear into dust in a matter of seconds, our clothes were off and scattered everywhere in the room.

Lou slowly moved his mouth from mine, trickling soft, unrushed kisses down my neck to the swell of my breasts. The warmth of his mouth on my skin sent a wave of unbridled sensations down to the tip of my toes. If this was the beginning of something wonderful and beautiful between us, I never wanted it to end. Just as I was reeling in my blissful thoughts, Lou gently bit on the tip of my taut nipple. Although it wasn't painful, it made my body jolt with pleasure. He exchanged the small nip with a soft, but very effective, swirl of his tongue, causing a surge of wetness to pool between my legs. It was only when his mouth completely surrounded the sensitized bud that my back came off of the bed, needing more of what he was offering

Feeling as though my body was going to burn with the tingling heat running through it, in a heated breath, I pleaded, "Please, Lou."

I had never seen a man move as quickly as Lou did. He practically jumped off the bed to grab his jeans. Pulling out a small packet from his pocket, he had it opened and the condom inside was sheathed over his engorged shaft in a matter of seconds. As I felt the heat of his body return as he laid next to me, he lowered his mouth to mine, resuming where he had left off moments ago. While his lips were doing magic on my mouth, his hand slid down my body, stopping just shy of my wet throbbing sex. Working against his hand, I needed to feel him inside me. Taking my cue, he dipped his finger inside my moistened channel and began moving it slowly in and out. His movements were driving me crazy as I began to circle my hips to get more friction.

Knowing that he could feel my desperation, he continued to tease me with his slow movements. Once again,

I pleaded, "Lou," before his finger curled just enough to hit the spot within me to make my body shudder with pure ecstasy. Never had I come with such force. When my body finally relaxed, he lowered his head to my ear and whispered, "Now you will get what you asked for."

The warmth of his hand left, but only to be replaced by the demand of his cock as he slowly began working it inside me. As he gently eased inside, I could feel my walls begin to stretch to accommodate his size. Spreading my legs wider, I wanted to feel all of him. Having him fully buried outweighed the pain as he pushed deeper and deeper. I wanted this, I wanted him.

Pushing my legs against my chest, Lou took hold of my arm and placed it above my head, using it as leverage as he continued to thrust deep inside me. I wanted so badly to wrap my arms around him, but when he took hold of my other arm and placed it above my head and held me there with one hand, I knew he had control over me. Just the thought of being at his will made my walls tighten, sending me in a free fall as I could no longer hold the pleasure wanting so desperately to be freed. In a soft whisper, he proclaimed, "This is us, Emma. Just like this."

~****~

The hot spray of water on my body felt wonderful. Every muscle began to relax. Being ordered to take a shower was something that I had no problem with. What was going to be even better was the meal that was waiting for me, satisfying the appetite I had worked up. Rinsing the last of the conditioner from my hair, I grabbed the soft plush towel from the rack and wrapped it around my damp body. Wiping the steam from the mirror, I looked at myself in the mirror to find a different woman staring back. I didn't feel like that helpless girl who was brought up on the streets of Manhattan. I felt more confident than I had ever felt before.

"Emma, breakfast is ready, babe," I heard Lou say through the bathroom door.

"I'll be there in a minute," I responded, liking the way he referred to me as 'babe.'

Heading out of the bathroom, I found my bag next to the dresser and placed it on the bed. Searching for something to put on, I finally decided on a pair of yoga pants and a tank top. Placing my hair in a messy bun, I headed to the kitchen, where I knew a delicious meal would be waiting for me.

As I entered the kitchen, Lou was on his cell looking like he had lost his best friend. The second he turned toward me, I realized that he was holding my phone in his hand. At first I was confused as to why he would be talking on my phone, but then he walked over to me and said, "That was the Red Oak Nursing Home. It's your mom. She's been taken to MacNeal Hospital in Chicago."

My heart fell to my stomach. Walking to Lou, I took my phone from him and swiped the screen. I couldn't believe that Red Oak would be calling and I needed to see for myself. Bringing up the recent calls, there it was, their number. Looking over to Lou, I asked hesitantly, afraid of what he would say, "What happened to her?"

"They said she had a seizure. We need to go, Emma," he declared.

We were out of the apartment and on our way to Chicago, Illinois, within a matter of minutes. I was so ridden with worry that it didn't even occur to me that it was going to be a twelve-hour drive. All I could think about was my mom and what could have caused her to have a seizure. I knew that Lou was also concerned. Not so much for my mom, but for me. I caught him looking my way several times before I finally said, "I'm okay, Lou."

"Everything will be okay with your mom, baby," he assured me.

"I know. I just need to stay positive. I just don't know what could have caused this."

"Maybe they will know more by the time we get there." Lou replied.

The drive to Chicago was pretty pastoral considering the events leading up to the trip. The only conversation was the cussing that Lou did at the drivers who either cut him off or wouldn't move over to the other lane so that he could pass. He had been driving so fast, I thought for sure that he would end up with a speeding ticket.

Eleven hours and thirty-eight minutes later, we pulled into a parking spot at MacNeal Hospital. Entering the emergency entrance, I headed to guest services and asked,

"Please, can you tell me where they have taken Carolyn Atwood?"

The lady at the desk began typing away at her computer. When she found the information that she was looking for, she looked to Lou and said, "Carolyn Atwood is in ICU, room two. It's on the third floor."

The minute she told us my mom's location, we were on our way to elevator. It seemed like it took forever to move. I always thought that time was of the essence in a hospital. Finally stopping on the third floor, we saw the sign that said ICU and headed down the hallway, which took us down another. Coming to two large wooden doors, we picked up the call phone and waited for someone to answer on the other end. As soon as we told them who we were, the wooden doors began to open

Lou was the first one to the nurse's station. I was looking in the rooms trying to spot my mom. She wasn't in any of them. Running up to the nurse's station, I placed my hand on the counter and demanded, "Where is Carolyn Atwood?"

The nurse behind the desk was not very happy with my demand. I could tell by the tone in her voice. "Ma'am, you need to chill out. Ms. Atwood is down in radiology getting a CAT scan. She should be back up in a few minutes. You're welcome to wait in room two for her."

Feeling remorse for my rudeness, I apologized, "Sorry for being so rude, but this is my mom."

With a half-smile the nurse replied, "Understandable."

While we waited in my mom's room, I couldn't help but wonder what the equipment was for and if all of it was for my mom or was standard for the ICU. Taking a seat in one of the hospital chairs, I waited for them to bring my mom back to her room. Lou was outside the ICU, trying to get a hold of Jagged Edge to let Peter know where he was. We had left so fast from Manhattan, and Lou had driven like a maniac, so he didn't have a chance to call anyone. His only concern was getting me here so that I could be with my mom.

Everything about this room seemed so sterile and kind of creepy. It felt as though this was the final place a person came to before they died. I hadn't been to a hospital since my mom was put in the nursing home. Even back then, I thought for sure that the hospital was going to be the last time I was ever going to see her. Trying to think positive, I stood from my seat and headed out the glass doors. I couldn't stay in that room any longer, but most of all, I couldn't stay in there alone.

Walking past the nurse's station, I opened the heavy wooden door, hoping that I would be able to find Lou without going too far in case they brought my mom back to her room. Walking to the waiting area, I spotted him sitting on one of the leather sofas talking on his cell phone. I walked over to him and took a seat beside him. The spot he had chosen to sit at was in perfect line with the hallway and I would be able to see them bring my mom back. Waiting patiently until he got off the phone, I decided to occupy my time by looking through one of those frilly magazines sitting on one of the end tables.

I heard the elevator, which was also close by, and waited for whomever was inside to come into view. I could see that it was two orderlies pushing a gurney and what looked to be a doctor following behind. Rising to my feet, I placed the magazine on the sofa and headed in their direction. Even though I hadn't seen my mom for some time,

I would recognize her anywhere. She didn't look too well and she had some kind of tube coming out of her mouth with some kind of machine at the foot of the gurney.

Following them through the wooden doors, I looked over to Lou to find that he was still on the phone. Whatever he was talking to Peter about, it must have been pretty important. I wished that he would hurry and end his call so that he could go inside with me while they got my mom settled. When the double wooden doors closed, I knew that he was going to probably be a while.

Staying out of the way, I waited until they had my mom off of the gurney and onto the other bed before I entered the room. I tried to stay out of the way as much as possible while the nurse, who followed us in, started hooking my mom up to the various monitors and equipment. If I didn't know better I would have thought that she was dead instead of unconscious. When the nurse was finished with what she was doing and all of the monitors began to light up and begin beeping, I knew that my mom was alive. Concentrating on the green line that went up and then dipped down, I wasn't aware that the doctor had spoken. "Excuse me, Miss, are you related to Ms. Atwood?"

Diverting my attention from the monitor to him, I answered in a soft voice, "I'm her daughter."

"Can we step outside of the room for a moment?' he asked.

Waiting for me to go through the glass doors, he soon was out of the room himself. Taking a deep breath, I asked the ultimate question. "Is my mom going to be okay?"

Before he could answer, Lou came through the double doors, diverting his attention. When Lou was finally by my side, the doctor looked at me and said, "I'm afraid not. Given your mom's history and the fact that she had sustained blunt force trauma to the head from a past assault, her brain at this moment is showing no signs of activity."

"But she is alive. The machines are showing that she is." I argued.

"That is only because we are keeping her alive. I can't tell you what to do, Miss Atwood, but I am afraid that once we remove the ventilator, your mom will not survive and will ultimately die. Right now, I believe it is the only thing keeping her alive. We can keep her on it for a couple of days, but after that, it will need to be removed."

I knew that the doctor was only doing his job, but I hated what he said. My mom was lying there and being kept alive by a damn machine. I only had one question for him. "What are the chances that she will be able to breathe on her own once you remove the ventilator?"

"Slim to none, I'm afraid. With the type of seizure she experienced, and the amount of time that it lasted, the damage done to her brain is irreversible. It would be a miracle if she was able to survive," the doctor advised.

I felt like I was living a nightmare. My mom was the only person I had left in my life. Even though she hadn't been with me for a long time, she was still my mom. Watching the doctor walk away, I slowly made it back inside my mom's room. Lou was right beside me. As soon as her condition hit me and the tears began to fall. Lou pulled me into his arm. Living on the streets and having that feeling of hopelessness was a day at the park compared to how I felt at that very moment.

CHAPTER FIFTEEN
Gainer

There were so many things that I wished I could do for Emma. Even though I had so many unanswered questions about her, it could never compare to what she had gone through the past couple of days. Since her mom was the only family she knew, Emma thought that it would be practical to have her cremated. I will never forget the look in Emma's eyes yesterday, when she told the doctor that she was ready for her mom to go in peace. It was a matter of minutes before her mom's body finally shut down after the ventilator was removed.

Today, we were on our way back to Manhattan. Me, Emma, and what was left of her mom. Emma said that her mom loved Central Park and that was where she felt her mom should be. She said that at least now when she walked through the park on the way to work, she could always visit her mom at the Balcony Bridge.

Driving home, even though just as quiet as the trip out, was not rushed. I was at a loss for words and wasn't sure if Emma was in a talking mood anyway. There was so much that I needed to tell her, but dealing with the death of her mom was all that she would be able to handle. Sharing what Peter had told me just wasn't an option at this point. It would crush Emma knowing that while we were in Chicago, another friend of hers was killed. There were only four girls plus Emma that went to Surge the night the first girl died. With only her and Courtney left, our time was running out to find the killer.

The only lead we had this time was that the killer left a note, **'PLATES OR ANOTHER ONE DIES.'** Even that wasn't enough since whomever left the note was smart enough to leave no prints. Currently, our only lead was Walsh McGowan. He had to be the answer to this, only we didn't know how.

Turning down Fifth Avenue, I found a parking spot across the street from Central Park. I suggested that we get some rest and come by in the morning to pour Emma's mom's ashes in the water below Balcony Bridge, but she insisted it had to be done right way.

This time of night was not the best time to be walking through Central Park. Too many bad things happen in the park at night. It seemed like all the misfits came out, causing havoc in the park. Holding tightly to Emma with one hand while holding onto her mom's ashes with the other, I kept my eyes open for any trouble. When we finally made it to the Balcony Bridge, I handed Emma the small box where her mother's ashes were kept. Removing the plastic, I watched as Emma pulled the container holding the ashes from the box. I knew that this was very hard for her. I regretfully moved away from her to give her some privacy. I could only hear bits and pieces of what she was saying as she poured the ashes into the water. It took everything I had not to go to her and pull her close to me.

When she turned to face me, her eyes were red with despair and she just looked at the empty box like her whole had been taken away from her. Unable to stand it anymore, I walked over to her and took her into my arms. In a small whimper she cried, "I am really going to miss her."

Kissing the top of her head, I pulled her even closer. "It will get better with time, baby," I assured her.

I couldn't have been more at ease when Emma decided it was best for us to head back to the truck. Even though the path we took was lit pretty well, the area around us was very dark. Holding her as close as I could to my body, I increased my pace, wanting more than anything to get to the safety of my truck. Seeing the exit of the park, I thought for sure we were safe, at least until I felt something being stuck in my back.

"Give me what I want and you live," a gruff voice said behind me.

"I have no idea what it is that you think I have, but my wallet is in my back pocket," I replied as calmly as possible. The only thing I could imagine he wanted was money.

"I don't want your fucking money, asshole. I want the fucking plates."

Everything was beginning to make sense. This guy, whoever he was, may have been the reason those innocent girls died. Stepping back with my left leg, I pushed Emma away from me and bent my body over just enough to throw this guy off balance. Twisting my body around, I was able to get behind him and force the gun out of his hand. Bringing him to the ground, I held him there with my knee in his back and demanded, "Who are you working for?"

"I'm never going to tell you. Do you think I'm stupid?" he answered between gritted teeth.

"Well, maybe you need a little incentive," I seethed, pulling my phone from my back pocket.

Looking over to Emma to make sure she was okay, I waited for Peter to answer the phone. When he finally picked up, I grunted, trying to hold the guy in place, "Gonna need your help, bro. I think we may have found our first lead to the deaths of those girls. He may need a little convincing. Can you get a hold of Ash and let him know to meet us at the shop?"

"Ash is still with Juliette in Hawaii. He won't be back until tomorrow. I'll get in touch with Chavez. He'll be able to do a little convincing," Peter suggested.

"Okay, we should be there in fifteen minutes," I declared.

"We?"

"Yeah, Emma is with me. See you in fifteen."

Ending the call, I looked at Emma and asked, "Emma, I need you to grab his gun. It fell in the grass."

Holding the scumbag to the ground, I waited for Emma to bring me the gun. When she handed it over, I grabbed the guy by the collar and brought him to his feet. I was glad that we weren't far from the truck. The last thing I needed was for this lowlife to pull a quick one.

As we got closer to the truck, I dug in my pocket and gave Emma the keys. "There is rope in the back, behind the back seat, I need you to get it for me. Can you do that, baby?" I asked.

"Yeah," she replied, walking ahead of me to the truck.

As Emma handed me the rope that she had pulled from behind the seat, I gave the gun to her while I began tying his hands behind his back. Placing him in the back seat, I finished tying him up by binding his feet together. Taking the gun from Emma, I said to her, "You will need to drive. I will let you know where to go."

Looking at me with anxiety, Emma confessed in a small voice. "Lou, I don't know how to drive."

This was something I didn't figure on. Of course, she wouldn't know how to drive. Handing the gun back to her, I advised, "Emma, you need to sit in the back with this scumbag. Don't take your eyes off him. Most importantly, if he tries anything, shoot him in the leg. We need to keep him alive."

Taking a few minutes to show Emma how to use the gun, I climbed in behind the wheel and pulled away from the curb. It was a good fifteen minutes to the shop, and that was assuming that traffic would be light. I hated having Emma watch this guy, but I had no other choice. Looking in the review mirror, I could tell that Emma was nervous about holding a gun to this guy by the way her hand was shaking. Getting her attention, I asked softly, "Baby, are you doing okay?"

"I'm okay, Lou. Just hurry. This guy is giving me the weebie jeebies," she replied, placing the gun in her other hand as she rubbed her hand against her jeans.

"Ten more minutes, baby."

When I pulled up to the shop, I had my door open before I turned off the engine. I needed to get this guy away from Emma as quick as possible. Opening the door, I grabbed the guy by the collar and dragged him out of the truck. Emma held the gun on him until I could untie the rope that I placed around his ankles. The guy almost got the best of me. Thankfully, Emma must have seen what the guy was about to do. She placed the gun to the guy's head and warned, "Don't try it, dickwad."

Smiling up at her, I took the gun from her and moved out of the way so that she could exit the truck. Before we got to the shop door, Peter opened it and held it open for us. Just as we passed him, he informed us, "The back room is all ready for our guest. Chavez should be here shortly."

The guy tried getting away, but was unsuccessful. Sitting him down on the metal chair, I secured his hands to the back of the chair and his ankles to the legs. There was no way this guy was going anywhere. Emma was still standing in the doorway like she was afraid to enter the room. She probably wanted to stay as far away from this guy as possible.

Just when I was about to tell her to wait in the lounge area, she walked away and Chavez walked through the door. I was never so glad to see a person as I was then. Holding my hand out to him, he began doing his signature handshake. Bumping shoulders, I said, "Nice to see ya, bro."

"Likewise, Gainer," he replied, looking over my shoulder. "So, this guy needs a little persuading."

"I think you're going to have your hands full with this asshole. Let me know if you need anything," I offered.

"Not so fast, bro. You're going to help me." Chavez declared.

Normally he would have wanted this guy all to himself, but when he told me to assist, there was no way I was going to refuse. Nodding my head, I said, "Be right back. Let me get Emma settled first."

Feeling like Emma would be okay in the lounge area, I headed back to the back room to assist Chavez in his interrogation. Opening the door, Chavez was already doing his thing, so I just stepped back and crossed my arms at my chest and let him take the lead.

I had to admit, he knew exactly what he was doing. The minute he took the guy by the hair and cocked his head back, I knew he wasn't going to mess around with this guy. His mouth was inches from his ear when he said, "Now, unless you want to lose that ear, you are going to tell me who you work for."

This guy was pretty loyal to whomever he was protecting. He didn't even budge when Chavez threatened him. His only response was to spit in Chavez's face when he looked him in the face for his answer. It didn't seem to faze him though. Chavez just wiped it away and gave a loud chuckle before he planted his fist across the guy's face. I guess that was one way to get the guy's attention. Amazed by the failure of his technique, Chavez looked over to me and said, "Looks like he is going to need a little more encouragement."

"What do you have in mind, bro?" I asked anxiously.

"See that bucket over there? Fill it full of cold water. I have a feeling he is going to tell us everything we need to know by the time I get done with him." Chavez grinned.

Grabbing the bucket that he was talking about, I headed out of the room to fill it full of water. It would also give me a chance to check in on Emma. She had been through a lot the last couple of days. It amazed me how strong she was. Making a detour, I headed to the front of the shop where she and Sly were playing a game of pool. Setting the bucket down. I walked over to where she was standing and asked, concerned, "How you doing, baby?"

She must have thought I was asking her about the game when she said, "Getting my ass kicked."

"Had I known Sly was going to talk you into playing pool, I would have warned you." I confessed as I looked over to Sly. "What are you doing here, anyway? Don't you have a gorgeous woman waiting for you at home?"

"Nah, girl's night out. Nikki isn't going to be home for at least another hour," he stated as he took a shot at the eight ball and ended up missing it completely.

"Well, don't beat her too bad. I have to get back to our guest."

I was glad that Sly was around to keep Emma company. Playing pool with her was one way to keep her mind off of everything that happened. Heading to the kitchen, I placed the bucket in the sink and began filling it with cold water. I had a pretty good idea what Chavez had in mind for this loser. Maybe when he began fighting for air, he would spill his guts.

CHAPTER SIXTEEN
Emma

I had never been so scared in my life. The minute Lou asked me to take the gun and aim it at the guy, I thought I was going to lose my lunch. It wasn't like I had never seen one before, but to actually hold one and aim it at a person was way out of my comfort zone. It was only after we reached Jagged Edge Security that I was finally able to breathe.

Not for long; the man standing at the door to the shop was just as gorgeous as Lou. Holding the guy by the collar, Lou introduced me to the hot guy. "Emma, this is Peter. He's the founder of Jagged Edge and the guy that is going to help us find out what happened to your three friends."

At first I thought that maybe Lou may have been confused, but Peter stepped in and replied, "We are going to find out who killed them, I promise you that."

Rubbing my head, I looked over to Lou and asked with confusion. "Another girl died?"

"I wanted to tell you, Emma, but with everything that was going on with your mom, I thought it would be better to wait," Lou admitted.

"Who was it, Lou?" I asked hesitantly.

"Her name was Heather Ingram," he said.

"Oh, my God," I cried, grabbing onto the door frame to balance myself.

Peter, reached out to steady me while Lou held on to the scumbag. I had never felt as helpless as I did that very moment. Everything around me was beginning to fall apart and I had no idea why. Looking over to Lou, I cried out, "Why? Why would anyone do this?"

"I don't know, babe, but we are going to find out. One way or another," he promised as he pulled on the guy's collar.

I followed the guys into the shop, which looked more like a mancave than a place of business. Off to the left side of the room was a lounge area with a couple of couches and a big-screen TV. That seemed pretty normal, but of all things, a pool table was centered in the middle of the room. The further we got inside, the better I was able to see. There was a large room that looked to be a conference room and another room that was clearly someone's office. Down the hallway there were several other rooms, one being a kitchen. The other I wasn't sure about, since the door was closed. Heading towards the back of the shop, there were several other doors which were closed. Lou opened the last door and dragged the guy inside. The room was empty except for an old metal chair, which was sitting in the middle of the room. This was clearly an interrogation room of some sort, based on the lack of furniture.

Waiting by the door, I watched as Lou placed the guy on the chair and began securing his hands and feet to it. Satisfied that he wasn't going anywhere, Lou walked over to me. Just as we were ready to leave, another hot guy walked through the door. *"OMG. Is being hot and gorgeous one of the requirements to work here?"* I thought to myself.

"Emma, this is Mike Chavez. He is one of the brothers that works here," Lou said as he introduced us.

"Nice to meet you," I replied.

"Likewise, doll," Mike responded, with an added wink.

I knew I didn't want to stay in that room and watch what Mike was going to do to that guy, even though it crossed my mind, but only because I would be in the company of two hot guys. As Lou held my hand, I followed him to the front of the shop, where he suggested I make myself comfortable. He wasn't sure how long it would take for them to get the information they needed from this guy. Sitting on one of the leather couches, I grabbed a magazine from the coffee table and watched as Lou headed back to the room where the guy was being held. Almost wishing that I was at Lou's sleeping in a warm comfortable bed, I dropped the magazine on the table and stretched out on the couch. As soon as my head hit the small pillow, my eyes closed and I was out.

Crack! Plop! I was up in a full sitting position, startled by the noise coming from behind me. Looking over the back of the couch, there was yet another hot guy playing a game of pool by himself. I knew that as long as he was playing there was no way that I was going to be able to sleep. As I pushed from the couch, a look of surprise crossed his face when he saw me. Holding the pool cue in confusion, he asked. "Where did you come from?"

"I was trying to sleep on the couch when you woke me up," I admitted, crossing my arms over my chest.

"I had no idea there was anyone else here. I'm Sly, by the way," he said, wiping his hand on his jeans before holding it out to me.

Walking over to him, I placed my small hand in his large one and replied, "Nice to meet you. My name is Emma. I'm a friend of Lou's."

"Cool. Can I interest you in a game of pool?"

"I've never played before," I said, embarrassed.

"No problem. All you have to do is use the white ball to hit the other balls in the pockets. What goes in on the break will tell you which balls are yours, either solid or stripes. The eight ball is neutral and is the winning shot, so make sure you hit that ball last," Sly instructed as he held up a solid-colored ball and then one with a stripe around the center.

"Okay, sounds simple enough. Who does the break thing?" I asked.

"I will, so you know what it is."

After Sly broke the balls, which were lined up in a pyramid, I watched him dunk ball after ball into the pockets on the table. When it was my turn, I focused my shot on the blue striped ball, but managed to miss it completely. I was really beginning to hate this game.

Two games later, I was completely frustrated and was about to call it quits when Lou came walking down the hall holding a bucket. I think more than anything he was surprised to see Sly at the shop instead of with his wife. Placing my cue on the table, I followed Lou like a long-lost puppy. When we got to the kitchen, I stood by the doorway and watched as Lou filled the bucket full of water. I wasn't sure why he was doing that, so I asked curiously, "What is the water for?"

"Mike is going to use it to persuade that dirtbag to talk," he said.

"Can I go with you? I've had about enough of getting my ass kicked," I mentioned.

"It isn't something that you need to see, Emma. It could get pretty intense in there. It's late, how about I have Sly drive you home and I'll see you later?"

"NO! Absolutely not." My tone may have been a little overboard based on Lou's reaction as he backed up with one arm in held in a surrender position.

"Okay, baby. But not a word, and if it gets to be too much for you, promise you will leave."

Doing the universal "cross my heart" gesture, I nodded and said, "I will. Cross my heart."

I stayed behind Lou as we walked toward the back room where the guy who held all the answers was being kept. I should have been concentrating on what was about to take place, but the only thing that occupied my mind was the way

Lou looked in his jeans. Two weeks ago, I wouldn't have thought twice about a guy's ass, now it seemed like that was all I thought about, at least when it came to Lou.

Channeling my thoughts elsewhere, I tried to think about something else. It became easier the closer we got to the room, as the sound of someone in excruciating pain came from behind the door. When Lou opened the door and we stepped inside, it was now evident as to why the guy was making so much noise. By the looks of his face, if I had to guess, Mike wasn't getting anywhere with the information that he needed.

Staying as far away as possible from what was taking place in the middle of the room, I propped my body against the wall and just observed what was happening without so much as a peep. Keeping my eyes focused on Lou and Mike, I watched as they tipped the metal chair back until it was lying flat on the floor with the guy facing up. Mike pulled a rag from his back pocket and placed it over the guy's head. When Lou handed Mike the bucket full of water, I had a pretty good idea what was going to take place.

Tilting the bucket until the water was running out, Mike held it over the guy's face, causing him to choke on the water. It was almost like they were trying to drown him. It wasn't until Mike righted the bucket and the guy caught his breath that I knew he was trying to make him talk. I guess the rag over the guy's head was to ensure that he wouldn't know when to hold his breath before the water came. After several attempts, the guy finally said, "Stop, I'll tell you everything you want to know."

"Who do you work for?" Lou demanded.

"I don't know for sure. I have never seen his face. He meets me in a black Cadillac and hands me instructions. The only thing I know for sure is that he is an older man and every time we've met, he's been wearing a gold ring with a ruby the size of a small country on his ring finger," the guy confessed.

I wasn't sure if what the guy said meant anything, but Lou's face turned as red as the blood dripping from the guy's face. Lou looked over to Mike and said, "I need to talk to Peter. You good here?"

Taking me by the hand, we left the room and headed back down the hall. I was so confused that I didn't know which way was up. Pulling against him, I got Lou's attention enough to make him stop. "What is going on, Lou? You look like you're about ready to whomp on somebody."

"There is something I need to take care of. I am going to have Sly drive you home," Lou said as he pulled me in for a hug.

"Wait. No, you don't. You don't get to do this, Lou. You can't just look like that and shove me onto someone else. Tell me what is going on," I demanded.

"I can't. Not yet."

~****~

When Sly pulled up to Lou's apartment building, he turned off the engine and sat for a minute staring out of the windshield. Grabbing the handle to the door, I was ready to get out when he said, "Gainer wanted me to make sure you got in okay."

"How thoughtful of him," I said sarcastically.

"Emma, whatever the reason, Gainer had to have me take you home. You need to trust him," Sly advised.

"Well, he needs to trust me and tell me what is going on." Not only annoyed by Lou's actions, I was beginning to get really pissed off.

Finished with this conversation, I opened the door and headed to the entrance to the apartment building. When I pulled on the door, I realized that I didn't have the key to get in. My only option was to wait for Sly to open it for me. I guess I shouldn't have flown off the handle. Now it was just embarrassing, and keeping my eyes to the sidewalk was the only way I was going to be able to get through this.

As we headed up to Lou's apartment, I tried to think of something to say, but I was at a loss for words. I was thankful when the doors open to Lou's floor. Sly signaled for me to go ahead while he fumbled to find the right key. When we got to the door, Sly opened the door and looked over to me. "Wait here for a minute while I check it out."

I didn't know what the big deal was. The guy they wanted was back at the shop and there would be no reason that I or Courtney would be in danger. Peeking my head in through the doorway, I wondered where Sly was and what he was doing. *"Probably checking under the bed for the boogie man."* I thought to myself.

When he finally appeared, he handed me the keys and said in a strong voice, "All clear," like I was one of the guys.

Exchanging spots, with me now on the inside of the apartment and him in the hallway, I turned and grabbed his arm, which was nothing but muscles, and said, "Thank you."

With a wink to show his awesomeness, he replied, "Lock the door, Emma."

Closing the door, I engaged the deadbolt and also the lock on the door knob. Pulling on the door to make sure it was indeed locked, I turned and headed to the bedroom. There was a king-sized bed calling my name. Thinking that I should let Lou know that I was home, I pulled my cell from my pocket and found his number. Sending him a quick text assuring him I was safe, I removed my clothing and got under the covers. I knew that Lou would be home soon, but that didn't stop me from stealing his pillow and holding it to my chest. Taking in his scent, the comfort of his smell eased me into a deep, serene sleep.

CHAPTER SEVENTEEN
Gainer

It was like a ton of bricks just came crashing down on my body. As soon as the dirtbag mentioned the ruby ring, I knew exactly who he was referring to. I knew what Father O'Malley was capable of, but I guess I never thought he would be capable of doing something so cold-blooded as to order that those innocent girls be killed in such a manner.

While Chavez was finishing up with our little stool pigeon, I need to talk to Peter. It was time that I let him know everything about my past so that we could put this motherfucker behind bars. Making sure that Emma was safely on her way to my apartment, I walked directly to Peter's office. Knocking on the door, I could see that he was just about ready to take off. Before he could leave, I asked, "Peter, got a minute? We need to talk."

"Sure, make it quick, though. Lilly and the girls are on their way home from girl's night out," he answered.

"You may want to sit down for this," I suggested, waiting for him to take a seat before I began. "I know you don't know much about me and my past before we served together, but I think it's time that I let you know about my childhood."

"You don't have to tell me anything, Gainer. I know enough about you to know you are a good man, and I consider you a brother," Peter jumped in.

"I need to do this, Peter. It has to do with the dirtbag in the other room." Telling him the truth about my past wasn't going to be easy, but I knew that it would help find O'Malley. "When I was a baby, my mom left me on the steps of an orphanage in Chicago, a Catholic orphanage, to be exact. Father O'Malley was the head of the orphanage, and let's just say he paid extra attention to the little boys that lived there."

"Wait, are you saying what I think you are?" Peter asked, concerned.

"Yeah, but I wasn't the only one. There had to be at least five of us that he put his hands on."

"I'm so sorry, bro. No wonder you never told anyone," Peter said sympathetically.

"I never thought that my past would come back to haunt me, but when our guest mentioned that the guy who ordered the hits on those girls was wearing a ruby ring, I knew exactly who he was talking about. I will never forget that damn ring. Every day that I was in that hellhole, he made us kiss that ring like he was some kind of savior." Stopping for a moment to gather my thoughts, I took a deep breath, and continued. "He's in New York and he is here for more than just an ordainment."

"So, you've seen this O'Malley guy?"

"Yeah, in the park. He was getting too close to a little boy so I stopped him. The funny thing is, he had no clue who I was. I also did a little checking. I had to know what he was doing in Manhattan. That was when I found out about the ordainment at St. Peter's. The priest I talked to said O'Malley had to leave on some sort of emergency in Chicago. I now know he's still here. He wouldn't leave knowing he had things to take care of."

"Wait a minute," Peter said, turning his attention to his computer. "I know that name."

I sat and waited for Peter to find what he was looking for on his computer. When he angled the computer screen my way, I couldn't believe what was before me. It was an article about Father O'Malley and McGowan. There was a picture of them together shaking hands. O'Malley in his dress clergy cloak, and McGowan in a designer suit.

"So, they knew each other. That explains a lot. We just need to find out what their connection was." Taking a closer look at the pic, I realized that the building behind them was St. Peter's. "Peter, I know that church. I think we need to find out what connection they have to St. Peter's."

"Not tonight, bro. It's late and I need to get home to my beautiful wife." Peter shut down the computer and headed out. Me, I just sat there for a minute to gather my thoughts and try to piece this shit together.

~****~

Everything was dark when I opened the door to my apartment. I knew exactly what I needed and headed in that direction. I was trying to be as quiet as possible, but trying to find my way in the dark made that impossible as I kept bumping into the furniture or a wall. When I finally made it to the bedroom, Emma was kind enough to have left the light on in the bathroom.

Kicking off my shoes and clothing, I headed in the direction of the light. Hearing a ruffle of the sheets, I turned towards the bed and found Emma sitting straight up. Walking over to her, I sat on the bed and said, "Sorry to wake you, baby."

"You didn't. I've been waiting for you," she paused as she scooted closer to me. "Lou, what happened to you in that room?"

Taking her by the hands, I looked down at them as I held them in mine. "Remember when I told you about the orphanage that I was raised in, and the priest who headed it?"

"Yeah, I remember."

"His name is Father O'Malley and he is the one that had a stake in the deaths of your friends. I think he has something to do with the fake money found in the hotel.

Peter and I found an article about him and the dead guy. They knew each other, and he sent that dirtbag that pulled the gun on us to get the plates. The plates used to make that counterfeit money."

"Counterfeit," Emma replied in a shaky breath.

"Yeah. It's beginning to make sense," I said as I began putting things together. "I think the reason your friends were killed was because of those plates. Who more than anyone had access to that room?"

"I don't know, Lou," Emma stated, standing and walking away from me.

"Think about it, Emma. They were all maids that worked at the hotel. They had access to the room. You and Courtney had access too."

When Emma turned to face me, her face was as white as the sheet on the bed. I knew she was scared for her life, but now that we were getting closer to putting O'Malley away for good, it was even more evident. Moving closer to her, I placed my hands on her arms and asked, "Emma, what is it? We are going to get him."

"I know, I'm just tired," she replied.

"Let's get some rest. It's late, and tomorrow we are going after O'Malley," I assured her.

As we climbed into bed, I pulled the covers over us and pulled Emma close to me. Holding her in my arms, I knew then that I was going to do whatever it took to protect her. With her head tucked beneath my chin, I was able to take in her scent, which soothed the tensions of the day and allowed my body to relax as my eyes slowly fell closed.

~****~

I must have been more tired than I thought because when I opened my eyes and felt beside me, Emma was no longer there. Her side of the bed was cold, like she had been gone for some time. Rolling over, I looked at the alarm clock and saw that it was only 7:00 a.m., which meant I had only been asleep for four hours. Swinging my legs to the side of the bed, I picked up my jeans and pulled my cell out from my back pocket. Finding Emma's number, I counted the rings, hoping that she would answer. When the call went to voicemail, I knew I was wasting my time.

Slipping on jeans and grabbing a clean shirt from my drawer, I picked up my boots and headed out of the apartment. I had a pretty good idea where I would find her. Something happened to her last night, and her explanation of being tired was a way of keeping me from finding out exactly what that was.

As soon as I got in the elevator, I put my boots on while I waited for the elevator to stop. Getting to my truck as fast as I could, I got in and headed to the Park Lane Hotel. I probably could have gotten there faster if I had walked, but I didn't want to take the chance of having to come back to the apartment if she wasn't there and losing precious time.

Pulling up to the hotel, I had a funny feeling in my gut that I would find something terrible inside the hotel. When I walked up to the door, nothing was out of the ordinary as I pushed the glass door of the hotel and entered. Everything was pretty much normal. People were moving about the lobby, and the guest services desk was stacked up with guests, either wanting to check in or check out. Walking to the back of the building, I decided the best place to start my search for Emma was in the employee lounge.

When I opened the door, the only person there was Emma's friend Courtney, whom I remembered seeing at Surge the night the first girl got murdered. Walking over to her, I cleared my throat to get her attention. "Excuse me," I said, and waited until she turned around.

"Hi, you're Emma's friend," she stated.

"Yah. You haven't by chance seen her?" I asked.

"Not today. She called in about an hour ago. She said she had something to do and would be in tomorrow," Courtney replied.

Heading for the door, I turned towards her and said, "Hey." She looked up at me and I continued. "Thanks for the info."

Heading out of the hotel, I tried to think where the hell she would have gone. I knew she wouldn't be at the motel, since she no longer had a room there. The only other place would be at the bridge where she dumped her mom's ashes. Crossing the street, I headed into the park and down the walking path towards Balcony Bridge. There were so many things going through my head, but mostly all I could think about was Emma. If she wasn't at the bridge, I wasn't sure where she would be.

Even though there were a lot of people on the bridge, none of them were Emma, *"Damn woman!"* I cursed to myself. I thought for sure that she would have been here. After waiting half an hour hoping that she would show up, I finally gave up and headed to my truck. Once again, I began thinking about everything that had to do with Emma. I thought back to last night when she turned so pale. I thought back even further to the interrogation, and further yet to my run-in with her friend TJ. Nothing made sense until I came upon a woman scolding her little boy for throwing a fit about something. When she said, "Tommy, do you want a spanking?" that was when I realized how I knew Emma's friend. I could have kicked myself in the ass for not picking up on it earlier when I had my first run-in with him.

Walking double-time, I got to my truck and headed to the shop. I needed to do a little more research on this TJ. If I was right about my hunch, I knew exactly who he was.

CHAPTER EIGHTEEN
Emma

Shit, shit, shit! All I could think about was what the hell I was going to do. The minute Lou said that the money was fake, all I could think about was everything that could go wrong. For one thing, I spent at least two thousand dollars of that money. If they found out that the money was fake, my days of freedom were over. TJ stealing the money may have actually been a godsend, but now he would be in trouble.

The minute the sun came up, I was out of bed and on my way to find TJ. He needed to know that the money wasn't real. Hopefully he was filling me full of shit when he said the money was already gone.

Doing the best I could not to wake Lou, I grabbed my clothes and slipped out of the apartment. When I got off the elevator, I pulled my phone from my small bag and called TJ. Even though he was an ass the last time we talked, he needed to know the truth about the money he took. After the third ring, he finally answered. "TJ, we need to talk," I demanded.

"God, Emma. Do you know what time it is?" he hissed.

"This is important. It's about the money." I said.

"If you are trying to get it back, I told you it is already gone."

"Then you have even bigger problems, because the money isn't real," I barked. "Now, where are you?"

Heading out of the building, I caught a cab to where TJ said he would be. He told me to meet him at some hole-in-the-wall café in Brooklyn. Whatever in the world he was doing in Brooklyn was beyond me. It took nearly half an hour and twenty bucks to get to where TJ wanted to meet. Paying the driver, I closed the door and started towards the door of the café when my cell began to ring. Taking it from my bag, it was Lou calling me. There was no way that I could answer it. He would want to know where I was, and I just couldn't tell him.

I spotted TJ the minute I opened the door. I had to admit that he looked a lot better than he did a few days ago. Sliding in the seat across from him, I sat there looking at him as a waitress came by to take my order. "Coffee, please," I said, before she could ask.

The minute she walked away, TJ placed his hands on the table like he was some sort of negotiator. Looking at me with his beady blue eyes, he admitted, "I know about the money."

"What do you mean you know about the money?" I inquired, still not understanding what he was saying.

"Well, not at first, but the man I owed money to was very pleased to see it. Matter of fact, he even wanted to know where it came from," TJ confessed.

"What is going on, TJ? Why would he want to know that?" Things were becoming more and more confusing. If I found out that the person who owed me money was trying to pawn off fake money as real, I'm pretty sure I would be beating the crap out of them instead of wondering where it came from.

TJ moved from where he was sitting and joined me on my side of the booth. Placing his hand on my cheek, he asserted, "This could be our break, Ems. All we have to do is find out where the plates are that made the bills. I even got a pretty good idea where they might be, based on what he said."

"Are you fucking crazy? Why the hell would I help you find them?" I cursed, pushing him out of my space. "Who the hell is this guy, anyway?"

"Let's just say, someone that I have known for a long time. He helped me get off the streets and get a decent job. I would have never ended up on the streets had I listened to him in the first place. He was the only person that showed me any attention."

"What you do, TJ, is all on you, but I'm telling you, this is bad and you need to get as far away from this guy as possible. Even if he did help you get off the streets, is helping him worth your freedom?"

"I don't plan on getting caught, Emma. You should really think about it."

TJ lowered his head and placed his mouth over mine, or at least tried to. Pushing him away, I choked, "You can't do that, TJ."

"Why, Ems? I am pretty sure that you and I have more in common than you have with that mound of muscle you've been around. Does he even know that you live on the streets? Bet that would change his feelings for you."

"What are you implying, TJ?" I asked, perturbed.

"Just saying." he replied, with a shit-eating grin, before he stood and left the café.

When the waitress came back with my coffee, she informed me that the gentleman had already paid for it. I knew that it wasn't TJ because he didn't stop to pay for anything before he left. The only other gentleman that it could have been was sitting at the bar drinking his own coffee while reading a newspaper. He was an older man in his late fifties to early sixties. Throwing a ten dollar bill on the counter, he turned my way, and I could tell that he was some sort of priest by the clergy collar he was wearing. When he looked straight at me and tipped his head, I knew that it had to be him that bought my coffee.

Taking a sip of my coffee, I watched as he left the café, only to notice the ring on his left ring finger as he pulled on the door. I began choking on my coffee, causing me to cough uncontrollably. Every set of eyes was on me as I tried to control my attack. The only thing I wanted to do was get out of there. Grabbing my small bag, I ran for the door and headed for who knew where. I knew that I needed to get in touch with Lou, but in doing that, I would need to explain where I was, and my past. I had to think, and the only place to do that was in Central Park. I needed to see my mom.

~****~

I walked down the walking trail to Balcony Bridge, surprised to find that there were so many people out and about so early. When I got to the bridge, my eyes fell upon the one person that surprised me even more. Sitting on a bench watching the early risers pass by was Lou. He was looking the other way, so I hid behind a tree, out of sight. I just needed to get out of here before he saw me. Talking with my mom was just going to have to wait.

I didn't know what I was thinking. There was nowhere for me to go. Other than Lou's, I had no other place to go. Then I remembered what Lou told me last night. I actually did have a place to go. Heading out of the park, I didn't have enough money for a cab, but I could still take the subway to the New York Public library. I knew that they would have computers that I could use to find out more information on this Father O'Malley. If he had something to do with killing those girls, maybe I could find something out. It sure would make it a lot easier if I knew more about this O'Malley guy when it came time to tell Lou about my past and the money.

Pulling three dollars from my pocket, I paid the attendant for my one-way ride to the library. Hopping on the train, I found a seat next to an older lady who looked like she spent most of her life outside. When the train left the subway station, my phone began to ring. Pulling it from my bag, I looked down at the screen to see that it was Lou again. Knowing that sooner or later I would need to talk to him, I accepted his call and said, "I know what you're thinking," before he could say anything.

"All I want to know is are you okay and where you are at," he said with concern.

Feeling like I owed him an explanation, I replied, "I am on my way to the public library. We need to talk, Lou."

"Don't go anywhere, Emma. I am on my way."

I wasn't planning on going anywhere but there. I was on a mission and I was going to find out all I could about O'Malley. I didn't care if he was a man of the cloth or not, he was evil and he needed to pay for everything he did to Lou and those girls.

I was off the subway train the minute the doors opened. Heading up the steps, I took them two at a time so I could begin my research before Lou got to the library. I wanted to show him that I could be of use even if I had secrets that I was keeping from him. Even though I didn't know that much about computers, I knew that there would be someone in the library that I would be able to ask.

Getting to the top of the steps, I spotted the library right away. Running across the street to beat the traffic light, I was up the steps and inside the massive building that held so much history in a matter of minutes. Finding the librarian, I asked with confidence, "Can you show me where the public computers are?"

"Of course, right this way. Is there anything in particular you will be looking for?" she asked with a smile, in a quiet voice.

"Yes, I need to do some research on Catholic churches and priests. It is for school," I answered, satisfying the curious look she had on her face.

When she pointed me in the right direction, there were already several people looking up information. I took a seat between a young girl who couldn't have been much younger than me and an older gentleman that looked like he should have been in a nursing home. Trying to figure out how to turn on the computer, I felt around the back for some kind of switch. I was just about ready to lift the keyboard from the table when the young girl pressed a button on the monitor and the computer came to life. Smiling over to me, she said, "These things can be a little tricky."

When the screen came up, I had no idea what to do next. Turning to the girl, I asked, "Can you help me get to where I need to be to look up information?"

"Sure," she said, without questioning my ignorance.

When the Internet came up, I plugged Father O'Malley's name in what she called the search engine, and waited for the information to pop up. Looking at the links, I tried to figure out which one was going to be the best. Having had little to no education, except what I learned living on the streets, I slowly read them until I found one that I could actually understand. There it was, as plain as the hair on my head, a picture of the man. The same man that was in the café. The same man who bought my coffee.

As I tried to read and understand the article about him, it seemed he was some important guy. It also seemed that he had his hand in everything that connected with the Catholic churches. He also seemed to be a very popular man amongst the people. Scrolling down the information, if I hadn't been reading the article so slow, I might have missed the information on Walsh McGowan. He and Father O'Malley had a strong connection to each other through the charitable contribution this McGowan made to the churches.

Continuing my search, I heard a sexy voice behind me. "Finding anything good?"

I just about jumped out of my seat at the sudden interruption to my deep thoughts. Turning my body in the chair, I looked up to Lou and said, "You scared the crap out me," as I took a deep breath while placing my hand across my chest.

"Sorry, didn't realize you were so deep in thought," he apologized.

There wasn't a vacant seat beside me, so Lou remained standing while looking at the computer monitor. The old man must have found what he was looking for, because he got up out of his chair, placed his hat on his bald head, and gestured for Lou to take his place at the computer desk. When Lou sat down, just like me, he began doing research on O'Malley. Pointing to my monitor, I found McGowan's name and asked Lou, "Do you know who Walsh McGowan is?"

Watching Lou's reaction. I knew he knew exactly who he was. It was confirmed when he answered, "Yeah. He was the dead guy at the Park. Didn't you know him?"

"I had no idea that he was the dead guy," I replied.

"I just thought that since you worked there you may have known him," Lou implied.

"Not at all. We don't get to know the guest by name at the hotel, only room number," I clarified.

Finding that there wasn't any information on the Internet that Lou didn't already know, we decided to grab something to eat. Heading out of the library, we walked over to Lou's Tundra and got in. Lou pulled up to a small sandwich place thinking that it was a good place to eat and talk. I think more than anything he wanted to know why I had left so quickly this morning. I was beginning to have second thoughts about telling him the whole truth about my past. I knew I needed to, at the very least, come clean about the money and tell him the truth about TJ.

Heading inside the sandwich shop, we found a booth towards the back where we would be able to talk. As soon as our order was placed, Lou ordering a French dip and me ordering a BLT, I placed my hand on the table and blurted out, "I did something really bad, Lou."

Lou took hold of my hands and began rubbing his fingers across them. "Whatever it is, it can't be that bad, baby."

Trying to gauge his mood, I looked down out our hands and closed my eyes for a moment before I began from the beginning. "Courtney asked if I would help her clean the suite on the 46th floor. She didn't want to have to stay late, so I told her I would. She was cleaning the bathroom while I finished up in the bedroom. There was a briefcase on the floor and I accidently hit it with the vacuum cleaner. It popped open and well... there was so much money. I never should have done what I did."

"What did you do, Emma? "Lou questioned.

"Let's just say, I helped myself," I admitted, almost in a whisper.

"How much, Emma?"

His voice had changed to an uncomfortable tone as he pulled his hand from mine. Maybe this was a mistake. I couldn't even look him in the eye and tell him the amount. I knew it didn't matter. It could have been only one dollar and he would have been pissed off.

"It doesn't matter, I can tell by the look on your face." Rising to my feet, I looked over my shoulder as I walked away and said, "I'm sorry." It was the last thing I said before I was out the door and out on the streets, at least until I could find some place better to live.

CHAPTER NINETEEN
Gainer

There was no way that I could let Emma leave. Yeah, what she did was so wrong in so many ways, but I really cared for her, and I wasn't going to lose her because she made the wrong choice. Letting the waitress know that I would be right back, I headed out the door to catch Emma before she got too far. Seeing her down the street, I began running towards her and yelled, "Emma, wait! Stop, baby."

The minute she turned around, I could tell that she had been crying. When I was standing in front of her, I wrapped my arms around her and confessed, "It will be okay, Emma. Even though I don't agree with what you did, we will figure something out."

I could feel her head move up and down as she held me tight, spilling even more tears. I hated it when she cried. It tore me up inside seeing her so sad. Holding her at arm's length I lowered my lips to hers and kissed her gently.

Feeling her lips part, I slipped my tongue inside her warm mouth. Taking each other in, like we were the last two people on earth, I knew then that my feelings for Emma were much more than just caring about her. I was falling for her and in a big way.

Breaking our kiss, I said, "Let's go back to the sandwich shop before the waitress comes looking for me."

Emma let out a small giggle as we began walking back. I held her close to my side, when she said, "I am really sorry. I've kind of made a mess of things."

Kissing her on her head, "No matter how bad, Emma, we will get through this together," I reassured her.

When we got to our table, our sandwiches were already on the table waiting for us. As we began eating our lunches, Emma told me the whole story about the money, where she spent it, and who took it. I knew that I didn't care for her friend TJ, but I didn't tell her that I actually knew him from the orphanage and that he was so shy back then. I guess you never know how a person's past can affect the way they live later on.

"What are we going to do, Lou?" she asked frantically.

"I think the best thing to do right now is to finish our lunch. Always better to think on a full stomach."

I needed to do whatever I could to get Emma's mind off of TJ and O'Malley. I just couldn't believe that the boy I once knew as Tommy Porter was mixed up in this. As much as I hated to admit it, he was going to be the key to everything. O'Malley must have had something over him in order for him to want any affiliation with him. The thing that worried me the most was the fact that O'Malley now knew about Emma. He was there at that café for a reason. If I had to guess, it was to keep tabs on Tommy and hopefully find out where his plates were. I was pretty sure that Emma didn't know anything about them. I also believed that the only person who knew for sure where they were was Walsh McGowan, and he was in no position to tell anyone.

Finished with our sandwiches, I paid the waitress and we headed out of the small eatery. We had a short distance to walk to my truck, and all I could think about was, *"What was it about this whole thing that didn't make sense?"* For one, why the hell would Tommy be involved with O'Malley, with everything that he did to him? There was also still the question as to who killed Walsh. The money was left in the room, so whomever it was knew that the money was fake. Tommy told Emma that he knew the money was fake, but that could be because O'Malley told him. And the plates, where the hell were they? One thing for sure: O'Malley was willing to kill to get them. One thing I knew for sure was, I needed to find out where O'Malley was and bring him in.

Helping Emma into the truck, I closed the door and decided then that the best way to get to O'Malley was through Tommy. As much as I hated it, the only way to do that was for Emma to contact him and set him up. Putting the truck into drive, I made an illegal U-turn and headed for the shop. I knew that I would need the help of my brothers to put a plan into place.

~****~

Pulling up to the shop, there were three vehicles in the front, which I knew were Peter's Camaro, Sly's Jeep, and Cop's black Ford truck. Heading inside, there was no one out front, which led me to believe that they were either in the back or in the conference room. Walking down the narrow hallway, I could see that no one was in the conference room, nor Peter's office. The only other place they could be was in the back. Going to a door adjacent to the room where we interrogated out little stool pigeon, I opened the door to find the guys busy cleaning weapons, with Chavez taking inventory.

Walking in the middle of the room, I put my fingers between my lips and blew between them to let out a loud whistle. I was surprised the guys even heard me with the radio playing *"Wanted, Dead or Alive"* full blast in the background. When Peter walked over to the radio and turned down the volume, that was what got the guys' attention.

"What's up, Gainer?" Peter asked, wiping his hands on a shop rag.

"Got some information for you guys, but mostly, I am going to need your help," I confessed.

"What's up?" Sly asked, leaning against the wall.

"Okay, so we know after talking to the stoolie in the interrogation room that the guy who ordered the hit on Emma's friends wore a ruby ring. What you didn't know is that I know who he is. His name is O'Malley and he's a priest. I think that he had something to do with McGowan's death and the fake money. So, here's the funny thing about this. Emma has a friend, whom she went to school with, whom I also know. He goes by the name of TJ, but his real name is Tommy Porter. He approached Emma with a proposition to help O'Malley find the plates they used to make those bills." I paused for a minute waiting for someone to respond. When I didn't get one, I continued. "This is what I propose. We set up TJ, or Tommy, and get him to lead us to O'Malley. It's the only way we are going to be able to get any information as to where those plates might be."

I tried to give the guys enough information without spilling Emma's mistake or how I knew O'Malley and Tommy. I think, most of all, they were willing to do whatever I suggested just to get this guy. Leaving the back, we all decided to take this discussion on what was going to be the best plan to the conference room. As we headed in that direction, Peter and I held back only because there was something on his mind.

"Gainer, do you have any idea how you want this to go down?" he asked in a low voice.

"I do. Even though I am not comfortable with it, I know it is pretty much the only option I have," I offered.

"Well, whatever it is, we are here for you," Peter responded.

By the time we went through what I had planned and ironed out some problems that we could run into, it was late afternoon. We had agreed that the best bet was for Emma to contact TJ and let him know that she decided to take him up on his offer to help find the plates. After the seed was planted, we would be right there to watch their every move. Sooner or later, O'Malley would be in contact with him. I knew this because he was the kind of person that preferred to handle his affairs in person. He didn't trust anyone, and he certainly didn't trust communicating by cell or email.

Entering the apartment after a long drive home, I went to the kitchen and poured myself a Jack Daniels while Emma went to take a long bath. Taking my drink with me, I sat on the couch and looked out the window to the city as the sun was just setting behind the tall buildings. As I sat there, I began going everything that had happened during the past couple of weeks, which brought me to my past. I must have been really deep in thought, because I didn't even hear

Emma come up behind me until she took a seat next to me and snuggled right up against my body. Moving my eyes from the window to her, I could only think of all the things I wanted to do to her at that moment, and with her only wearing a towel, that thought was just about to become reality. Placing my glass of Jack on the end table, I turned towards her and gently lowered her to the couch until she was on her back. Taking in her beauty, I took hold of the towel that was tucked between her perfect breasts and pulled it away to expose her creamy smooth skin.

Lowering my head, my mouth soon found her breast and I began caressing her taut nipple with my tongue. With my hand, I outlined her other nipple and circled it into a hard peak with my finger. Opening the towel completely, her beautiful perfection was before me, and I took it all in from the tip of her perfect nose, down to her firm breasts, her perfectly shaven mound, to the very tip of her toes. Working my way down her silky softness, I could feel the rise of her hips as the kisses I placed on her skin began to have an effect on her. Kissing her mound, I felt the warmth between my fingers as I slipped one and then two fingers inside her tight pussy. The warmth of her womanhood coated my fingers as I slowly glided them back and forth. I could feel her walls tighten, pulling my fingers deeper inside her.

Emma's hips began moving against my thrusts in circular motions all the while I was consuming her sweet honey. A moan of ecstasy filled the room as I continued my assault on her. Her scent filled me completely, making me crazy with desire for her. Unable to hold out any longer, I lifted her from the couch and held her in my arms as I carried her to my room. Removing my clothes, I checked my pocket for a condom only to come up short. "Shit," I cursed as I headed into the bathroom.

Returning with condom in hand, I sheathed my cock and lowered my body onto the bed next to Emma. God, she was beautiful. Her cheeks were flushed with need matching my own hunger for her. Placing my mouth over hers, I consumed her as she parted her lips for me, inviting me inside. As our tongues entwined together, her arms wrapped around my waist until she lowered them to my ass, pulling me even closer to her. I could feel the swell of her breasts against my chest, coaxing me to take her. The vibration of her moans just about had me undone as my hand fell between our bodies in search for her heat.

Sliding my finger between her moistened folds, I carefully dipped it inside, anticipating the feel of her warmth when I entered her with my throbbing shaft. Pushing to my knees, I took the packet I had been holding onto and ripped it open with my teeth, and resumed my assault on her plump lips. Sliding the lubricated glove over my hard cock, I positioned my body between her legs before slowly pushing against her entrance. The heat of her pussy hit the tip, causing me to dive in with glory. Her warmth consumed me as I thrust deeper and deeper inside her.

I needed to feel more of her. Taking her legs that she had wrapped around my waist, I lifted them one at a time and placed them over my shoulder as I angled her hips upward. Getting full penetration, my thrusts increased, and her breasts began swaying in sync to the force of my cock inside her.

When I heard her scream of ecstasy, I knew that she had reached the point of excellence as her body began to shudder with pleasure. When her walls began to tighten with her release, mine also was met as she milked my cock until there was nothing left. My body was fully spent and fell gently upon hers in utter bliss.

When I got back to the bed after dumping the aftermath of our moment of pure heaven, Emma was already asleep with my pillow nestled tightly to her chest. I didn't have the heart to wake her, so I went to the guest bedroom to get another pillow. On my way to the kitchen to get a quick drink of water, I heard a light knock on the door. If I hadn't come this way, I would have never heard it, it was that soft. Wondering who it could be, I looked through the peep hole to be ultimately disgusted by the man I saw on the other side. There was no way I was going to open this door in my current state of dress. Pulling the chain across the door opening, I latched it and opened the door just enough to say what I needed to. "What the hell are you doing here?"

"I need to talk to you."

"Whatever you have to say, I don't want to hear," I cursed in response.

"You're going to want to hear this."

"Hold on."

I was not ready for this, and I was pretty sure whatever Tommy had to say was nothing I wanted to hear, but given his persistence, he convinced me to hear him out. Heading to the bedroom, I gathered my jeans and slipped them on as I headed back to the front door. When I opened the door, I was even more surprised by what I saw. Tommy looked like he had been on a seven-day binge and hadn't seen a drop of water during that time. As he stepped by me to enter my apartment, he smelled to high heaven, like he lived in a sewer.

"Jesus, bathe much?" I asked, holding my hand over my nose.

"Very funny," he cursed.

"So, what is this about, Tommy?" I demanded.

"So, you know who I am. I wondered when you were going to remember me. Looks like you've done pretty well for yourself," he replied as he looked around my apartment.

"Say what you need to say, and then I think it is best that you leave," I responded.

"Figured you would say that. Just like in the orphanage. Did you even care about what happened to me after you left? I trusted you to stay with me. I thought we were going to get out of that shithole together. You have no idea what I went through," Tommy choked.

When he lifted his soiled shirt, I had to take in a breath to keep in my disgust. What kind of person would do this? His body was covered in large burn marks that looked as though someone had poured hot oil on him. "My God, Tommy. What happened to you in there?"

"If it wasn't for O'Malley, I would have died."

"Are you shitting me? He molested you, bro. Why would you say that?"

"Because if it hadn't been for him, my whole body could have been scorched with that torch, and I wouldn't be alive. Those boys got what they deserved, and O'Malley made sure they would never hurt anyone again. Do you know what they called me? A fucking fag cocksucker. There were four of them. Came in from juvie. They knew about O'Malley and how he loved little boys. Kept telling me that O'Malley was my girlfriend. O'Malley got wind of it. Not sure what happened to them, but after they burned me, they disappeared and I spent two weeks hidden away. O'Malley said they were troublemakers and got transferred. Me, I think he killed them. I had to get out of there, so when I had the chance, I ran. Been living on the streets up until nine months ago when Father O'Malley approached me with a proposition."

"Holy fucking hell. So, you didn't leave." I replied, shocked by what Tommy just said.

"Hell no. You did, though."

Our conversation must have woken Emma. I didn't hear her come into the living room until she asked, "TJ, what are you doing here?"

CHAPTER TWENTY
Emma

I had to rub my eyes twice in order to make sure TJ was in the living room with Lou. All I wanted to know was, why the hell he was here in the first place? Tugging at Lou's t-shirt that I had grabbed off the floor. I looked at Lou and then to TJ and asked, "What the hell is going on?"

Lou stepped up to me and lightly kissed my forehead and whispered, "We need to get some things sorted, and that means everything."

I had a funny feeling that TJ may have told him more than I wanted Lou to know. Looking up to Lou, I said in a soft voice. "I was going to tell you, but I was afraid that you would leave me. You're all I have, Lou."

"What are you talking about, Emma?" Lou questioned.

"My past. If I told you where I really live and how I knew TJ, I thought you would be disgusted with me and never want to see me again."

"Emma, I'm not sure what you're talking about, but I think it is time you explain."

"Emma, I didn't say anything to him," TJ protested.

It was then that I knew I just ratted out myself. There was no way I was going to get out of this. My only option was to come clean and tell Lou everything. Walking past him, I took a seat on the couch and pulled a pillow to my chest. I closed my eyes and took in a deep breath. "My mom and I haven't had the easiest of lives. I think she did the best she could, but somehow got mixed up with the wrong kind of people. Her choices were what landed us on the streets and ultimately led to her death. When she had to be taken care of, I knew I needed to do something. It was then that I got a job working at the Park Lane. The expense to care for her was so much that it took everything I made there. I wasn't able to afford a place for myself, so I continued to live on the streets. I didn't meet TJ at school, I met him on the streets."

"How many more secrets are you keeping from me, Emma?" Lou asked forking his fingers through his hair. "You should have been straight with me from the beginning. I need to think. I think it's best that you and your friend TJ, or Tommy, or whatever the fuck his name is, leave."

"Lou, please. You are all I have," I cried.

"Then you should have been honest with me. How am I ever going to be able to trust you? When I get back, I want you gone."

My heart fell into my stomach the minute Lou grabbed the keys to his truck and left the apartment. I just sat there hoping that this was all a dream. I thought for sure that after I explained to him what my life was like, he would have forgiven me for not telling him. I wasn't sure how much time passed by while I just sat on the couch in a daze.

TJ walked over to me and took a seat beside me, "Everything will be okay, Emma. We still have each other."

The minute he said those words, I knew that he only wanted me for one thing. He was never going to be my friend. He was going to use me to get what he needed, and then he would be gone too. "Just go, TJ."

"You don't mean that, Emma," he replied.

"I do. Please just go."

When he walked to the door and I heard it close behind him, I knew that the only person I could count on was myself. Just like the last fifteen years of my life, I needed to look out for me. Never again was I going to let anyone get close to me, just to have them taken away or leave. Getting up from the couch, I headed into the bedroom and began gathering my things. I had at least two hours before I needed to start my shift at the hotel. This was plenty of time to find somewhere else to stay. Knowing that I no longer needed to pay for my mom's care. I was finally able to think about myself and make a good life. I would never have to depend on anyone.

~****~

The atmosphere at the hotel was very quiet among the employees. I felt like it was my fault that those girls had to die. If I hadn't taken the money, they might still be alive.

Closing my locker, I headed to my maid's cart to make sure it was fully stocked. As I placed the last of the shampoo in the little tub, Delores came up to me and said, "I am going to assign you to the 46nd floor. It will be added to your schedule."

Nodding my head, I kept my eyes on the cart and said, "Sure, no problem."

Finishing my last room on the 39th floor, I pushed my cart down the hallway to the elevator. As soon as the doors opened, I pushed it inside and hit the button for the 46th floor and swiped my maid key. Stopping at the suite where Walsh McGowan was killed, I swiped my key card and pushed open the door. Walking in the room, I could see the large blood spot on the floor where he was killed. I just stood there trying to figure out why people were so malicious and had to kill someone for what they wanted. Sitting on a chair and staring at the stain, I began pulling out the drawers on the desk and looked down at the Bible that was inside the drawer. Lifting it from its spot, I opened it up and tried to read the words. Fanning the pages, something caught my eye; it was under the book of Peter.

Some of the words had been highlighted. It didn't really make sense why someone would highlight certain words. I could understand a whole passage, but just words, strange. A thought came to me as I picked up the small complementary note pad and pen. Jotting down the words as I came to them, I read what I had written. Even though I wasn't a good reader, I understood exactly what the words meant, *"In the holy Temple of God, St. Peter will guide you to the treasure through your confession."* Going to my cart, I took a Bible from my cart and replaced it with the one I knew I needed to keep. Closing the door, I headed to the rooms that needed to be cleaned. I wanted so badly to leave to test out my theory, but I knew that if I wanted to keep my job, I had to stay and finish out my day.

While I was finishing up cleaning my last room, I was thinking about all the things that Lou said to me. I knew that I should have been honest with him, but just as I thought, he left me. The only difference would have been that he would have left me two weeks earlier when I barely knew him and he hadn't captured my heart. The more I thought about it, if the words I found in the Bible were some sort of clue as to where the plates were, maybe if I could find some way get them and give them to Lou, maybe everything I kept from him would be forgiven.

Pulling out the piece of paper that I had written the words on, I knew that it had to do with St. Peter's church. As soon as I got off, that was going to be my first stop. Tucking the small piece of paper back inside my uniform pocket, I pushed my cart to the elevator and pressed the down button. As I waited for the elevator to arrive, I felt the vibration of my cell in my pocket. Looking at the screen, it was TJ. I didn't have the time nor the desire to speak with him. Declining the call, I heard the little beep letting me know that he had left a message.

There was no way that whatever he had to say was going to ruin my day any more than it already had. My focus was on getting to that church and finding those plates. According to what I had written, the only place they could be was where confessions were made, and having heard enough about it, that would have to be the confessional.

Placing my cart in the large supply closet, I clocked out and headed out of the hotel, only to head back inside because I forgot to grab my bag. Before I could open the glass door, I was greeted by the one man I had no intention of talking to. "I have nothing to say to you, TJ."

"I just wanted you to know that I didn't say anything to your boyfriend about your past. We were actually talking about mine," he divulged.

"What could you possibly share with him that he would remotely want to know? He beat the shit out of you, or have you forgotten?" I reminded him.

"Well, maybe your boyfriend hasn't been as forthcoming as you have. He and I knew each other in the orphanage I told you about. Matter of fact, he pretty much threw me under the bus when he left."

I had no idea what he was talking about. "You aren't making any sense, TJ," I said as I turned to head back inside the hotel.

"Lou Gainer and I were Father O'Malley's prize possessions, and when he left, there was no one else to protect me from the new boys that came shortly after."

"So, are you trying to tell me that Lou knows you from the orphanage, and he didn't say anything about it?"

"Yep. That pretty much sums it up."

"I really don't care if he knew you or not, because the way I look at it, I will never be able to confront him with it and you know why… because he is never going to talk to me AGAIN," I shouted as I pushed him out of my way.

"So, stay with me, Emma. You don't have to go back to the streets. I have always cared about you. Even when I got off the streets there wasn't a day that went by that I didn't think about you. I even followed you until I finally had the courage to confront you," TJ confessed.

"Wait. You've been following me?" I hissed, turning to face him.

"Not in the way you think. I did it just to make sure you were safe."

"Leave me alone, TJ. Go to O'Malley." I had to get as far away as possible from this man. I no longer trusted him. I didn't get the chance, because the minute I tried to cross the street and head into Central Park, since he was blocking the door to the hotel, a black sedan pulled up to the curb and the door flew open. I tried to back away from the car, but TJ was right behind me shoving me inside. Sitting in the backseat was none other than the man they called O'Malley. Fighting to get away, I was stopped when I felt a prick in my arm. O'Malley was holding a syringe and before I could say anything, everything went dark.

CHAPTER TWENTY-ONE
Gainer

As I began driving to who knew where, I began taking a hard look at my life and what it really meant. I had no right to treat Emma the way I did. My life was no better than hers and there were still some secrets that she didn't know about me. Like the fact that I knew who TJ was. Even though it was just confirmed, I should have told her that there was something about him that looked familiar. With everything that happened to him, I should have done everything I could to get him out of that godforsaken place. I really thought he left.

I had only one thing in mind that I needed to do. I just prayed that I wasn't too late. Turning around on a dirt road, I headed back to my apartment. I only hoped that Emma was still there and I could beg for her forgiveness before she left, despite me being gone most of the day. I pulled into my spot in the parking garage at my apartment building. When I finally opened the door to my apartment after an excruciating long elevator ride, I knew she was no longer there. Trying to stay hopeful, I went to look in the bedroom. No Emma. It was if she had never been here. The only evidence of her presences was the note that I saw leaning against the dark gray pillow on my bed. Unfolding the sheet of paper, I began reading her words.

Lou,

I know that I should have told you everything about myself, especially since you shared so much of yourself with me. I am so sorry that I hurt you. That was something that I had no intention of doing. I promise that I will do everything I can to make it up to you. I will never give up on finding the man who has taken so much away from you and me. I can promise you that. I hope that one day you will be able to understand why I kept my past from you and forgive me.

xoxox

Emma

Reading over the words, I tried to figure out what Emma was going to do. She didn't have much information to go on and I was afraid that she was going to end up getting herself killed. Pulling my cell from my pocket, I needed to get in touch with Peter and the guys. We needed to find Emma before she did something stupid.

By the time I got off the phone with Peter, everyone was on the lookout for Emma. I had a pretty good idea where she would be. My little drive cost me a lot of time and I needed to hurry if I was going to catch her at the hotel.

When I reached the Park Lane, the first place I went was to the employee lounge. Opening the door, I headed to where the lockers were, hoping to find Emma still here. When I came up empty, I went to Delores' office to see if she could tell me where Emma would be. When I got there, she wasn't inside. Running my hand through my hair, I realized I was batting a thousand as far as coming up short. Looking down at my watch, I knew that I was too late. It was already after five and I knew that Emma was long gone.

As I was leaving the employee area, Courtney was pushing her maid's cart through the door. If anyone knew Emma's schedule better than Delores, Courtney would. Moving out of the way to let her pass, I walked up behind her and asked, "Courtney, do you know where Emma is?"

"She was assigned to the 46nd floor today, maybe she is up there," Courtney shared as another maid came through the wooden door.

"Are you trying to find Emma?" the young maid asked as she walked towards us.

"Yeah." I replied. "Do you know where she might be?"

"It's the strangest thing. One minute she was arguing with some guy out front and the next she was getting inside a black car. It almost looked like she didn't want to go," she said.

"Did you see what the guy looked like that she was arguing with?" I asked.

"Yeah. He was kind of cute, tall, blonde, good build."

When she described the man that Emma was with, I knew right away that it was Tommy. What I couldn't understand was what Emma was doing with him, unless he planned on going through with his proposition without her consent. Heading over to the security office, I needed to find out if they had any footage of the conversation that took place in front of the hotel. Maybe the cameras even captured a plate number for me.

Walking past the check-in counter and past the employee lounge, I moved towards the end of the long hallway where the security room was. Knocking lightly on the door, I waited for someone to open it. A man dressed in a guard's uniform appeared who could have laid off the chocolate donuts, especially the one he had in his chubby hand. Wiping the chocolate from his mouth with the back of his hand, he asked gruffly, "Is there something I can help you with?"

"Yeah. My name is Lou Gainer. I work with Jagged Edge Security. I need to see your security footage from the front of the hotel," I commanded as I pulled my ID from my back pocket.

"Sure thing," he replied as he stepped to the side to let me enter.

Taking in my surroundings, there were four guys in the room, each looking at a monitor in front of them. Looking over to chubby, I asked with authority, "Can you please bring up the footage from today of the front of the hotel?"

"No problem," he said as he took a seat in front of a keyboard and began typing. "How far back do you want to go?"

"A couple of hours should do it." I was pretty certain that it couldn't have been that long ago that Emma was forced into that car. Keeping my eyes peeled to the screen, Emma leaving the hotel came up plain as day. The clarity of the footage was amazing. Normally, it was black and white and hard to really see the detail. When Tommy came into view, I knew that he wasn't far away. He had been waiting for her. It also looked like she wasn't the least bit happy that he was in her space, going by the way she pushed him away. How I wished they had audio on this footage so I could hear what was being said. When the black car pulled up, which looked to be a Cadillac, and the door swung open, I knew then that Emma was in trouble. My hunch was confirmed when Tommy guided her inside against her will. As the Cadillac pulled away from the curb, I could barely see the plate.

"Back it up to when the girl gets in the car and stop it when I tell you," I ordered.

I watched the footage again, this time more closely, I yelled "Stop," causing the guard to jump from his seat. Even though I wasn't able to get a clear view of the plate, I was able to get something much better. There in the review side mirror was the reflection of the man. I knew who was behind this: O'Malley. I had seen enough. Thanking the guys for their assistance, I headed out of the room and back to my apartment to get my truck.

Running through the park was like trying to go through an obstacle course. I had never weaved between so many people in my life. I had no idea why of all days, today people decided to visit Central Park. Pulling my keys from my pocket, I headed into the parking garage to get my truck. I knew that at least a couple of hours had passed since O'Malley had taken Emma. I had no idea what it was that he wanted from her, unless it had something to do with Tommy wanting her to help him find the plates.

Edging on to the street, I could feel the vibration of my cell in my pocket. Looking at the screen while merging into traffic, I could see that it was Peter.

"Peter, I am my way to the shop. O'Malley took Emma," I seethed before he could get a word in as to why he was calling.

"I know, he left a present at the shop. How far out are you?" Peter inquired.

"Ten, fifteen minutes tops," I replied, stepping harder on the gas pedal. "What did he leave, Peter?"

"You'll see for yourself when you get here."

I knew that it had to be bad if Peter was holding out on telling me until I got to the shop. All I knew was that if that son-of-a-bitch did anything to Emma, he was going to be a dead motherfucker, but even that would be too good for him, because he wouldn't be close to suffering the way I did all those years. No, he was going to pay. Killing him would be too good for him.

Taking a right down the road that led to the shop, I could see that most of the guys were already here by their cars being lined up in front. Parking my truck beside Sly's Jeep, I quickly turned off the engine and rushed to get inside.

There was no one in the front room, but I could hear voices coming from the conference room. With the amount of cussing going on, I knew that something was definitely up. Entering the room, I felt like I was the subject of their conversation as silence filled the room. When Peter walked up to me and handed me a box, I knew it was bad.

Before I lifted the lid, I heard him say, "I'm so sorry, bro."

Slowly removing the lid from the box, I pulled back the tissue paper, only to find a finger sitting in a pool of blood. "Jesus fucking Christ," I yelled as I closed the box, disgusted by the contents.

Looking to Peter he handed me a note. As I unfolded the piece of paper, my world just crumbled in front of my eyes. *'Next time it will be her head, if I don't get those plates,'* it read as I stared down at the words. The way Peter looked at me, he knew how seeing this affected me. Placing his hand on my shoulder, he said with assurance, "We are going to get him, bro. No way is he going to get away with this."

"So where do we begin? How do we get this motherfucker?"

~****~

It was late by the time we left the shop. We finally had a plan in place on how to catch O'Malley at his own game. Chavez, being the boy wonder that he was, came up with an idea that couldn't have been more brilliant. He said that he could find a way to fake the plates, at least good enough to trick O'Malley into thinking they were the real thing. With his mechanical skills, it would take no effort on his part to do it, especially with 3D printers to help.

I offered to help Chavez, but he insisted that he had it and that I should go home. Little did he know that I didn't know if I wanted to. Right now, more than anything, I wanted to find Emma, hold her, and never let her go. I think my feelings for her went way beyond the caring factor. I was falling for her, and harder than I cared to admit.

Sitting in my truck, staring out the front window, I played back in my mind the security footage at the hotel. Even though it was evident that O'Malley had taken her, something was off. The more I thought about it, the more frustrated I got, and then it occurred to me. The one thing that Emma always had wasn't in her possession. It was her damn bag. She carried that thing everywhere, and I was pretty sure her turning to go back inside the hotel wasn't to get away from Tommy.

Turning on the engine, I put the truck into reverse and backed out of my parking spot. I knew it was late, but I needed to get to the hotel and check Emma's locker. I was running out of ideas of where she could have been taken. Maybe there was something inside that bag of hers to help me find her.

CHAPTER TWENTY-TWO
Emma

I had no idea where I was when I came to, nor did I know what time it was. Wherever I was, it was dark and there was barely enough light to see my hand in front of my face. It almost felt like I might have been in a basement, by the cool dampness of the air. Pushing to my feet, I walked over to where the light was coming from underneath the door to see if by some miracle, the door would be unlocked. Reaching out in front of me, I wanted to be prepared in case there was something in my way.

When I got to the door, I pulled on the handle and hoped that it would open. Just my luck, it was locked. Turning my back against the door, I slid down it until my butt came to rest on the cold floor. I was so confused by everything that was happening. I had no idea why I was here or what TJ and O'Malley could possibly want with me. As I sat in the darkness, lost in my own thoughts, I could hear a man's voice coming closer. Pushing to my feet, I walked away from the door and waited for it to open.

Hearing the door being unlocked. I held my breath in anticipation of who might be on the other side. When O'Malley appeared on the other side, I backed away from him. He was with a much younger man who couldn't have been much older than eighteen. I did notice that he was rather large for his age. I tried to fight him off when he grabbed my arm, but it was no use; he was much stronger than me and was able to lead me out of the room. Still trying to get free, I cursed with a vengeance. "Where are you taking me? I demand you let me go!"

There was an annoying chuckle from O'Malley as he spoke. "You aren't going anywhere, at least not for now. Tell me what I want and that could change."

"I have nothing to say to you," I hissed, pulling against the tight grip the young man had on me.

"You will, my child. You will."

This asshole was so sure of himself. Whatever he thought I knew, he was sadly mistaken. There was no way I would ever tell him anything. The only person I would ever share what I knew with was Lou.

As we continued walking, I could tell that we must have been in the basement of some old church. The walls were made of stone, with inlaid shelving which held crosses and other statues that depicted religion. The further we went down the hall the lighter it got, which told me that the part of the basement we just left was rarely used.

O'Malley came to a stop and pushed open a door. He went in first and I was close behind as the young guy pushed me inside. The lights were already on and I could see the room they had taken me to was a library or study. As I looked around the room, there were shelves after shelves as high as the ceiling filled with books that appeared to be very old. In the center of the room were two couches covered in red velvet with a dark wood table separating them. On the other side of the room was a large desk with scrolls and maps lying on top. The whole room seemed a little medieval with all of the dark wood and candelabras that were standing on each side of the enormous desk.

Pulling on my arm, which I knew was going to leave a mark, the young man led me over to the couch closest to the large desk and ordered me to sit. Taking my place like a good child, I looked over my shoulder where O'Malley was now sitting behind the desk. My patience was beginning to wear thin as I asked rudely, "Tell me what you want?"

"What I have always wanted, child. Those FUCKING plates." His eyes were as dark as death as he choked on his words.

His voice was so loud and evil that I could the floor vibrate beneath my feet. Sitting tall on the couch, I had to let him know that I wasn't afraid of him. As long as he thought I knew where those plates were, I knew that he wouldn't kill me. Somehow, I had to convince him that I knew where they were and convince to let me go so I could show him.

Lying through my teeth, I said, "I will take you to them."

"Do you think I am stupid enough to have you show me where they are? You have five minutes to tell me where they are, or you will never see daylight again."

His words ran together as he pounded his fist on the hard wood. My heart began to jump as he walked from behind his desk to where I was sitting. Pulling me to my feet, I knew my time was up. "Wait. I'll tell you."

"Good, I'm glad that you have chosen wisely," he said with a grin.

I needed to buy myself some time. Instead of giving him the piece of paper I had stuffed in my pocket, I directed him to my locker, which I knew he would not be able to access without me. "I don't know exactly where your plates are, but there was a clue left in the suite where that man died. It was hidden in the Bible. The Bible is in my locker, and the only way you are going to get it is if I get it for you."

"If this is a trick, you will be sorry," he mocked, lifting my chin to show his authority. "Bring the car around, we are going for a drive."

~****~

Heading out of the old church, which wasn't a church, but some sort of home for children, I knew that we were no longer in New York. It was then that I realized that he must have taken me to the old orphanage where Lou and TJ were raised. The children playing in the courtyard were a dead giveaway. I would have yelled to them to run, only I knew that they would never be able to hear me, and if they did, it could be the end of me. Not saying a word, I followed O'Malley to the car and slid in beside him, where I was instantly cuffed to him. I knew that it was at least a twelve-hour drive back to New York, and sooner or later we would need to stop and get gas. It would be the only way that I would be able to get away from them.

We had been driving for hours and I knew soon we would be needing gas. My stomach was in knots trying to think of a way that I could escape from them. I could only pray that they would be stopping to fuel inside a town or city instead of out in the middle of nowhere, where there wouldn't be any place to run. Coming upon a small town, the driver turned off the main road and headed down the street where there was a gas station off to the right. When he pulled up to the pump and shut the engine off, I looked over to O'Malley and pleaded, "I really need to go to the bathroom."

I could tell by his body language that he was not happy with my request. Pulling a key from his pocket, he unlocked the cuff from our hands. Opening the door, he got out and rounded the back of the car to my side. Grabbing me by the arm and somewhat assisting me out of the car, he whispered in my ear with gritted teeth, "No funny stuff."

As we walked to the building, we both spotted the bathrooms, which were on the outside of the building. Walking me to the woman's bathroom, he turned the knob and looked inside the bathroom. I guess he wanted to make sure no one else was inside. Closing the door, he again whispered, "You've got two minutes."

Pulling my arm out of his grip, I entered the small room to find that there were two stalls. There, staring at me above the second stall, was a small window. This was my chance to get away. Stepping on the toilet, I undid the latch on the window and slid it open. There was a screen on the window, which I was able to remove by lifting the two tabs that were on the bottom. Almost losing my grip on the screen, I took in a deep breath and maneuvered it inside the bathroom. Placing it carefully on the floor next to the toilet, I stepped upon the back of the toilet and used all of my strength to hoist myself up to the opening. I knew that my two minutes were up, so I ran like crazy down the alley that was in the back of the station.

Hearing O'Malley's voice in the distance, I didn't have enough time to get far away from them. My only hope was to find a good place to hide. Taking a chance, I spotted a large dumpster, climbed inside, and carefully closed the lip. It stunk to high heaven, but I knew I needed to get under the garbage bags, out of sight. Squeezing my body under two bags, I plugged my nose and breathed through my mouth, praying that they wouldn't find me.

I hadn't heard anything for some time and knew that it was getting late. Moving the bags that I hid under, I carefully opened the lid to the dumpster, just enough to see if it was safe. It was almost dark, and as I looked around, there was no one in sight. Climbing out, I kept my body low as I hurried back to the gas station. I knew I had to be careful. If I got caught, it would not be good for me. Pressing up to the building, I took small steps until I got to the corner. Squatting down, I looked around the side to see that the black car was no longer at the pump. Even though I was pretty sure that O'Malley and the young man, whom I was certain was his plaything, were gone, I still wanted to make sure to stay out of sight, and that meant finding another place to call for help.

Turning in the other direction, I began jogging at a steady pace down the alley in search of another place where I could call for help. Reaching the end of the alley, I looked down the street and noticed a sign for a small café to the left. It was getting dark and I was probably wasting my time, but I had to find out if the diner was open. The minute I got to the door, I knew it was closed by the blue and white sign that was hanging in the door. There was a light on inside, giving me hope that maybe someone was still inside. Banging on the door, I could see some movement in the back. It was a woman. As she got closer, I saw she wasn't much older than me.

Waiting as she turned the lock, I moved back a step so she could swing the door open. "Can I help you with something, Miss?" she asked with a sincere smile.

"I really need to use your phone. I'm kind of in trouble," I confessed.

"Does it have to do with those two men who were here earlier? One of them was a priest. I could tell he wasn't a very nice one either," she pointed out.

"Yes, it does. I need to call my friend in New York. Collect, of course."

As she moved to the side to let me in, I walked passed her and waited as she locked the door. "This way, Hun," she indicated.

As I followed her through the dining area to the back, I took in my surroundings. This was actually a quaint little diner. I bet it was very popular among the older people, with the checkered tablecloths and the silk daisies in the glass vases that were on every table and along the bar. Walking through the steel swinging doors, the young girl pointed to the phone on the wall. As I picked up the receiver, I couldn't remember Lou's cell number. The only thing I could do was call the operator to connect me to Jagged Edge Security.

I was never so happy to hear the most amazing voice ever. "Lou, I need your help."

CHAPTER TWENTY-THREE
Gainer

Emma's voice was the sweetest sound I had ever heard. The minute she told me where she was and that she needed help, I was in my truck and on my way to her. She was less than eight hours away and all I wanted was to hold her in my arms. I hoped that she took my advice to stay out of sight until I got there. I figured the best place for her to stay was at the nearest motel. As soon as she got there, she was to have the manager give me a call so that I could pay for her room. I wasn't about to take any chances and come up short again. After I checked her bag that she left at the hotel and found nothing that told me anything, I was about to go crazy with worry. It was not going to happen.

As soon as I got out of the city and onto I-90, it was smooth sailing with my speed just under 80 MPH. As much as I wanted to get to Emma, I knew that a speeding ticket would only slow me down. I told her to check in with me as soon as she got settled in her room. When my phone began to vibrate, I knew that it had to be her.

"Emma, are you okay?" I asked, keeping my eyes on the road.

"Yes. I'm in my room. I'm so sorry about everything, Lou. I should have told you everything," she sobbed.

"It's okay, baby. I shouldn't have reacted the way I did. If I didn't, all of this may not have happened and you would still be safe in New York, with me."

"I have something to tell you, Lou. It's about those pla....."

Before she could finish what she was going to say, the call dropped. I couldn't believe that this was happening right now. I looked at my phone several times hoping that at least one bar would come up so that I could call her back. I could turn back around and stop until I got my bars back, but I didn't want to waste any more time. I just needed to wait until the signal came back.

I was beginning to get impatient. I must have driven at least sixty miles and still nothing. Just when I was about to give up and take the next exit where there were services to make a call from a payphone, my signal came back. Getting to my recent calls, I pressed the little receiver icon and waited for her to pick up. After the fourth ring, I knew she wasn't going to answer. If I hadn't been worried before, I was worried now.

~****~

Pulling up to the motel where I knew Emma was, I parked in front of her room and quickly got out of the truck. Banging on the door, I frantically yelled, "Emma. Open the door."

When she came into view, with only a towel barely covering her body, I wrapped my arms around her and pressed my lips to hers. The feel of her in my arms was all the comfort I needed to settle my mind. Breaking our kiss, I pulled away and held up her hands to make sure she had all of her fingers. Taking her in my arms again, I said, "I was worried. You didn't answer when I called you back."

"When the call dropped, I figured you must have lost your cell signal. All I wanted to do was take a shower. Do you know how rank garbage is in a dumpster?" Emma replied.

"No, I guess I don't," I answered with a chuckle as she pinched her nose with her fingers while she waved the other back and forth.

"That's not funny, Lou. It was the most disgusting thing I have ever had to do, and having to live on the streets, I've had to do some pretty disgusting things."

"Well, all of that is going to change. You will never have to live that life again," I declared.

I knew by the look on her face that she had no idea what I was saying. Picking her up and carrying her into the motel room, I whispered in her ear, "Because you are going to live with me."

Her eyes began to water. I brushed a tear from her cheek and placed my mouth over hers. Even though the taste of salt from her tears managed to join our connection, it didn't matter. All I wanted to do was consume her, tears and all.

Placing her gently on the bed, I trailed open-mouthed kisses along the length of her neck. Stopping just short of her ample breasts, I hummed with contentment. "God, I've missed this," as my mouth captured her right nipple between my lips, caressing it gently with my tongue until it peaked into a hard pebble. Trailing kisses down the valley between her perfect globes, I worked my way to the other side, giving her other nipple the same attention. Her back curved as it rose from the mattress, giving me the full benefit of her beautiful breasts. Kneeling between her legs, I placed my hands on each calf and flipped her over gently onto her stomach. Sliding my hands up her silky thighs, I smacked her ass, not hard, but enough to cause her to gasp with pleasure. Kissing the small of her back, I pulled away her towel and placed my hands on her hips and guided her firm ass towards me so that she was on her knees.

Reaching inside my pocket, I pulled out a small packet before pulling my jeans off and discarding them onto the floor. Sheathing my engorged erection, I positioned myself at her entrance and slowly began rocking my hips in easy movements as I pushed inside her tight channel. The warmth of her vagina coated me like a blanket of velvety softness. Emma's walls began to contract, letting me know that she was close. Reaching around her, I lowered my hand to her clit and showed her what it meant to be fully pleasured as I began moving the tip of my index finger in circular movements around the hard nub.

Her hips began moving against my thrusts in perfect rhythm as I continued my assault on her clit. The sound of her moans escaped with the sweetest of words, "Lou, don't ever leave me."

Before I could make my promise to her that never again would I leave, her body began to shudder and I could feel her walls tighten around my cock. I drove deeper inside her until I too was met with my ultimate release that sent a stream of pleasure through my body all the way to my soul. Reveling in complete bliss, Emma's body collapsed to the bed, sending mine to cover hers. I knew my weight was too much so I slowly rolled off of her to rid myself of the condom that was coated with her essence.

When I returned to the bed, Emma had pulled the covers over her body and was sleeping soundly, like a baby that had just been fed. Climbing in next to her, I pulled her close to my side and kissed her gently on the temple. With an emotional surge, I took in her scent and whispered, "I love you, Emma."

It was only when she brought my hand to her lips and kissed it gently with a "Ditto" that I knew she was my freedom.

~****~

The morning couldn't have come soon enough, as I spent most of the night staring into the darkness. The nightmare of my past somehow crept in and took over my thoughts. I thought for sure that the nightmares that had been a part of my life for so long were finally gone forever. Taking my cell from the bedside table, I brought it to life to see that it was four o'clock in the morning. Just like every other morning, I would escape my torment by running, only this time I couldn't. There was no way I would leave Emma's side, so instead, I just laid in the bed and tried to gather my thoughts and think of something else, like how wonderful my life was going to be now that Emma was part of it.

When it reached 6:00 a.m., I pushed from the bed and tugged my jeans on before heading outside to call Peter. I knew he would be worried sick since I was too preoccupied last night to let him know that Emma was safe. The minute he answered, my assumption was confirmed.

"So, glad you found the time to let me know that you were FUCKING okay," he bellowed, none too happy.

"Sorry, bro. Time got away from me. Got a little preoccupied." It was the only thing I could say that I was pretty sure he would understand. "Listen, we are going to be heading out shortly. Just wanted you to know that we should be back in Manhattan before nightfall."

"Good, and Gainer, next time call first," Peter joked, letting me know he knew why I was preoccupied and couldn't call.

Going back inside, I looked over to the bed to see that Emma was no longer sleeping. Seeing that the bathroom door was closed, I knew that she was inside. Knocking gently, I asked, "You okay, baby?"

"Yeah. Be out in a sec," she replied.

When the door opened and she stepped out already dressed. I knew she was ready to get out of here and back to Manhattan. Straightening her dress, she placed her hands in her pockets only to pull out a piece of paper. As she handed it to me without a word, I unfolded the note and read it out loud. *"In the holy Temple of God, St. Peter will guide you to the treasure through your confession."* Looking up from the note, I asked, "What does this mean, baby?"

"When I went to the hotel to work my shift, Delores assigned me the 46th floor to clean. I decided to check out the suite where that guy was killed. It still hadn't been cleaned. I wanted to try and find anything that would tie O'Malley to those deaths, but most of all I wanted to help you. I'm not even sure why, but I took out the Bible from the desk and began fanning through the pages. That was when I saw those words highlighted. The same ones on the note. I think that it is a clue to where those plates are. I think they are at St. Peter's in one of the confessionals."

"You might be on to something. When we get to Manhattan, we will share this with Peter. If they are there, I want to be the one who finds them."

I had never kept anything from Peter, but the note that Emma gave me made perfect sense. It would be the perfect place to hide the counterfeit plates. I knew that if I contacted Peter with this information, he would be at the church in a heartbeat, and I wasn't going to miss out on finding them there. So, the best thing to do was to wait and tell him when we got to the shop, since that was going to be our first stop.

Heading to the truck, it hit me that I had grabbed Emma's bag from her locker. Helping her inside, I opened the back door and unzipped her bag, Emma looked at me with concern. "How did you get my bag?"

"After you left and I read your note, I went to the hotel to find you before you did something stupid. You forgot to lock your locker and your bag was sitting inside. I saw the Bible in there, but didn't think anything of it," I confessed as I pulled the black book from her bag and zipped the bag closed.

Taking my place behind the wheel, I thumbed through the pages until I came to the first highlighted word. Just like Emma said, the individual words were highlighted, which, when put together, gave us the clue we needed to find those plates. I could have kissed her for being so smart, and that was exactly what I did.

CHAPTER TWENTY-FOUR
Emma

I was antsy as hell as Lou drove down I-90 on our way back to Manhattan. The only thing that I wanted was for Jagged Edge to have those plates in their possession and O'Malley and TJ behind bars for life. As we got closer to town, I was about to burst with worry. Looking over to Lou, I asked hysterically, "What do you think Peter will do once you tell him about the plates?"

"The only thing he can do. Go to the church and get them."

"But what if O'Malley and TJ are there?" I questioned.

"The only reason they would be there is by coincidence. There is no way they know where those plates are. If they did, they wouldn't have kidnapped you." Lou's words were sharp and cold, as though he would kill them if he had the chance.

When we got the shop, the cars were lined up in front just like before. Assisting me out of the truck, Lou held my hand and squeezed it gently as he opened the door. The guys came into view right away. They were all waiting in the lounge area with mutinous looks on their faces. It was as though they were ready to fight a war.

"Hey guys. Things are looking up," Lou began, my look of confusion searing into his face. "We may have a lead as to where those plates are."

As Lou began explaining to the guys where the location of the plates might be, the guys were hanging on every word. The more Lou talked, the better I could tell that Mike Chavez and Sly were already trying to piece how they could get the plates. By the time Lou finished, a plan was in place to get the plates, and with my help, get O'Malley to the church, along with his sidekick TJ. I wanted to do more, but Lou insisted I wait at the apartment until everything was over. There was no way I was going to do that. With a little convincing, I was able to talk Lou into allowing me to go, but waiting outside the church until everything was clear.

With the plan in place, I made the one phone call where I knew I was going to have really work my charm. Using my own cell, I dialed TJ and waited for him to answer. When his voice came over the speaker, I said, "I know where the plates are. Tell O'Malley to meet me at St. Peter's."

"Hold on. What make you think I believe anything that you are saying?" he coughed.

"Because I know where they are and you pretty much don't have any choice but to believe me." I had to admit, I was even beginning to believe myself.

That was, until I heard, "Listen, child, this is how it is going to be. We will not be meeting at St. Peter's. Instead, we will be meeting at St. Andrew's and you will come along. The minute we feel any deception on your part, well, let's just say you will be looking over your shoulder every day of your life until one day you won't have to because, my child, you'll be dead. Tomorrow at noon," O'Malley cursed before continuing. "One more thing, don't be late."

All Lou had to do was look at me and I knew this meeting wasn't going to happen, at least not with me. "There is no way that I am going to risk Emma getting killed by this asshole. Nikki is about her size and has the same hair color. We can send her."

"One problem, bro. If O'Malley has any suspicion that something isn't right, Emma is going to be in danger for the rest of her life. We have to go through with sending her. It is not to say that we won't be close by, out of sight," Peter pointed out.

Peter was right. There was no way that I wanted this hanging over me the rest of my life. I didn't want a life of constantly looking over my shoulder. The best thing to do was go through with the meeting and pray everything would go as planned.

~****~

On the drive home, Lou didn't say one word to me. I felt like he was blaming me for what needed to be done. I wasn't sure what I could say to him to make him understand that I had to do this. Turning to face him, I could no longer hold back what needed to be said. "Lou, you must know that this is the only we are going to be able to TJ and O'Malley. If at any point they see that anything is wrong, I might as well dig my own grave. Sending Nikki is sure to guarantee that."

Pulling the truck to the side of the road, he put the truck into park and brought my body over the center console and pressed his lips to mine. It just about took my breath away the way he took hold of me. Never had I felt so much passion from him. When he broke the kiss, he rubbed my cheek with his thumb and vowed softly, "I love you, Emma. You are everything to me and I will always keep you safe."

His words were so sincere. Nobody had every professed that kind of compassion for me. Even though I knew deep down my mother loved me, she never did anything to keep me safe. I was her protector. I was the one who watched out for her, took care of her. Placing my hand over his, I looked deep into his eyes to absorb all the love they held and muttered, "I know," before I pressed my lips to his.

If it hadn't been for the fact that we were pulled over to the side of the road, I would have showed him just how much. I took my place back on the passenger side, Lou put the truck into drive, and made his way back onto the road. As darkness began to take hold of the day, I kept wondering how tomorrow would play out. Then I began to worry about the words that were highlighted in the Bible and the hint they revealed. What if we were wrong and the plates weren't where I thought they would be? What if the clue meant something else?

Feeling like my mind was going to combust, I let out a loud, "Urrr!" causing Lou to slam on the breaks.

"Baby, are you okay?" he wailed with an expression of worry on his face.

"I just wish I knew for sure that those plates were in that church. What if they aren't there, Lou?" I said, doubt running through my mind.

"Emma, they will be there. Where else could they be? The clue was pretty cut and dried. There is no other St. Peter's Church in Manhattan," Lou said, reassuring me as he took hold of my hand. His eyes shifted to the road as he began driving again.

I didn't say another word until Lou pulled into the parking garage, and even then, it was only one-word sentences. When we entered the apartment, Lou took my bag to the bedroom while I got something to drink. Reaching into the cabinet, I pulled down Lou's bottle of Jack and two glasses. I wasn't much of a whiskey person. Matter of fact, I wasn't much of anything since my first experience with alcohol a few weeks ago. Pouring us each a generous amount, I carried the glasses over to the couch. Taking a seat, I placed Lou's on the coffee table while I kept mine close. With a few sips in me, I could feel my body begin to relax. Downing the rest of my whiskey, I stood to get another shot, only to be greeted by Lou, who was standing behind the couch.

Something was going on with him. His cell was in his hand and the look on his face said everything. Something bad happened. Getting his attention, I asked, "Lou, what is it?"

"Courtney, she didn't show up for work this morning and they can't reach her on her cell. Ryan and Chavez are headed to her place to see if she is there. It may be nothing, but if I had to guess, O'Malley had something to do with this."

"Why wouldn't he have said anything earlier when I talked to him?' I asked, concerned.

"Because he is a lowlife asshole and probably didn't want to give away his insurance policy that you would come alone," Lou cursed.

"This is all my fault," I cried as I fell to the couch.

"This in no way is your fault, Emma. That man is a sadistic bastard."

Rounding the couch, Lou was beside me and pulling me close to him. He always managed to find a way to make me feel better. I didn't know what I would do if I ended up losing Courtney. She was the only friend I had. As much as I loved Lou, there were just some things that only a woman would be able to understand.

There was a comfort that washed over me as we sat in silence, just staring out the window at the magnificent skyline. I could feel the pressure of his sweet lips press against my head as he spoke in a soft but reassuring tone. "Everything will work out, Emma. O'Malley and TJ will get what they deserve."

Shifting in his arms. I turned to face him, finding his face contorted with hate and disgust. Easing my hands up his chiseled chest, I met his eyes and lifted my lips to meet his. His tension eased and his arms swept along my back as he slowly lifted the hem of my t-shirt up my back and over my head. The warmth of his breath felt as light as a summer breeze, making my body vibrate with a need I had never wanted before. With no objection, he laid me gently along the length of the couch and slid my leggings down my thighs, taking my not-so-sexy panties with them. As I laid there in anticipation, I watched as he quickly removed his jeans. When his beautiful maleness came into view, my body began to tingle just knowing soon he would be inside me.

As he ripped open the packet that he took from his pocket before placing his jeans on the floor, my eyes were focused on his ridged member as he expertly rolled the glove over it. Feeling the tips of my hard nipples rub against his hard chest, the friction alone had me undone. I knew that I was ready for him and all I wanted was to feel him inside me. But more than that, I wanted to one day feel his warmth with nothing between. Just me and him.

Towering above me with a grin that told me I was his, he slowly eased inside my channel. Flesh to flesh, man to woman, our bodies became as one, in perfect sync with each other's. Lou pushed to his hands and with an expression that only a person in love could understand, he lowered his head, placing his lips over mine. My emotions took over and my gates opened, releasing the pleasure that was only meant for him. Reeling in my delight, Lou increased his movements, pumping harder, with more eagerness, inside me. I was certain that my body was going to explode with ecstasy. I waited as long as I could to control yet another release, until Lou screamed with contentment, finding his own paradise. There was nothing I wanted more than to be here with him, like this, forever.

CHAPTER TWENTY-FIVE
Gainer

It was late when I woke up scrunched next to Emma's warmth on the couch, which was not meant for one person, let alone two. I was able to roll off the edge and get to my feet without waking Emma. Her hands were curled up under her head as the rest of her body was extended out. With only a small blanket covering her, I was blessed to see the curves of her silky legs and the way the softness of her skin beamed from the lights of the city shining through the window.

I was so mesmerized by her beauty that the fact that my body was sore from sleeping in such a contorted position didn't seem to bother me anymore. Gazing down at her, I knew that lying in the bed would be more comfortable than sleeping on the couch. Wrapping her body in the blanket, I slipped my arms under her body and lifted her. A small moan escaped as she nestled her head in the hollow of my neck. With a small whimper she asked, "Where are we going?"

"To bed, baby," I said as I placed a kiss on her head.

"Mmmm, that's nice," she muttered, snuggling even closer to my body, causing my will to take her again to be tested.

Pulling the covers away, I gently lowered her onto the mattress and rid her of the small blanket. Gazing down at her beauty for a minute, I covered her with the comforter even though I could have stood there all night, memorizing every curve and line of her perfection.

Taking my place beside her, I drew her near to me and wrapped my arm around her soft body. My thoughts began to drift to what my life would be without her and how frightened I was about tomorrow. Not for myself, but for her. Even though I would do everything in my power to protect her, there was still the possibility that something could go wrong. If O'Malley did have Courtney and was using her as leverage to make sure that he got what he wanted without any incident, then her life could very well be in jeopardy as well. The more I thought about it, the more I knew we needed to spread the coverage. We needed to split up. Even though Emma was to meet him at St. Andrew's, I believed that men covering St. Peter's would no doubt benefit the plan. It would assure that the men would be ready for O'Malley once he got there.

Unable to think anymore, because my head was beginning to hurt and my eyes felt like lead, I kissed Emma on the head and fell into a deep sleep.

~****~

"Get the fuck away from me. I'm not going to let you touch me ever again. You're never going to touch anyone ever again." My eyes burst open and my body was drenched in sweat. Looking over to Emma, I thanked God that she was still asleep. These fucking nightmares were going to end up having the best of me. This shit with O'Malley needed to end.

No longer able to sleep, I had to do the only thing that I knew would be able to clear my mind. Swinging my legs over the side of the bed, I slipped on my running shorts, grabbed my shoes, and looked back at Emma before closing the door. It was so early that I was pretty confident that I would be back long before Emma would be getting up. Just to be safe, I jotted down a few words on a note and wrote a whole bunch of 'xoxox' under my name. I knew that girls liked that kind of stuff.

Heading out of my apartment, I couldn't believe that even at 5:00 a.m. it was already warm. Increasing my stride, I jogged across the street and into the park. Already people were up doing their thing. It never ceased to amaze me how early Manhattan came alive. I guess that is why I loved this city so much

After getting a good burn in my lungs, and a clearer mind, I decided to do something special for Emma. Heading over to the best bagel shop in New York, I figured a good breakfast would do Emma good. Reaching the little shop, I pulled out my credit card and ordered two cinnamon crisp bagels with apple-honey cream cheese and two coffees to go.

I guess I should have requested a drink cart for the coffees. I didn't realize how hard it was to juggle the hot cups while trying to unlock the door. Emma must have heard me from inside the door because just as I was about to place them on the carpet, the door opened with my beautiful Emma standing on the other side. Handing her one of the cups, I said with a big smile, "Morning, sunshine"

Grabbing the cup, she smiled back. "The x's and o's were a nice touch."

"Yeah, I thought you might like them." I was right, girls did like that sappy stuff.

Taking our bagels to the kitchen, I pulled them out of the bag and placed them on a plate. Emma, wearing only one of my shirts, which I could get used to, took a seat at the bar and took one of the plates and began spreading the cream cheese on one of the halves. When she licked her finger to remove the excess, my eyes focused on her lips as they curled around her finger. It was almost too much for me and the erection that was growing between my legs.

The minute her eyes met mine and she batted her eyelashes at me, I knew that she was playing with me. She certainly knew what made me hard. Then again, it wasn't that difficult when it came to her.

Finishing what seemed to be a flirtatious breakfast, I only wanted one thing, and that was her, but I also needed to shower. Killing two birds with one stone, I lifted her from her seat and slung her over my shoulder. The view was amazing as the t-shirt she was wearing was no longer hiding the cute little ass that was going to be mine. With a little giggle, she asked, "Where are you taking me, handsome?"

"I think you may have missed a spot of cream cheese. I thought I would help you with that."

I knew she was well aware of where I was going to take her so with all love behind it, I smacked her on her tight little ass and continued to smile at what was going to happen in that shower. The cream cheese on her lips wasn't the only thing I was going to be licking.

Setting her down carefully on the tiled floor, I reached inside the shower and turned the water on. Helping her rid herself of my t-shirt, I couldn't help but dip my head to her breasts and capture her pert nipple in my mouth. Emma lowered her arms and slid her fingers inside the waistband of her panties and lowered them to the floor. I, of course, couldn't resist kissing her on her mound before lifting her to the counter before I continued. There was nothing sweeter than to taste than her sweet honey. I so loved when she was ready for me. Giving her sex the attention that it needed, I stopped my ministration, but only because if I didn't, we would never be getting our shower.

Removing my clothes, her eyes were upon me waiting with anticipation for me to finish what I had started. Kissing her on the lips, my hands fell to her ass and cupped her tight cheeks as I lifted her from the counter and carried her to the shower. Once inside, the feel of the water cascading down between our bodies was all it took as the water beaded on her firm breasts. The pressure inside me was almost unbearable as my cock stood at full attention.

Pressing her body against the cool tile, her whimper sounded as she moved her hands to my shoulders to steady herself. The air in the shower began to thicken, coating the glass with steam. Taking what I knew to be mine, I lowered my lips to hers and parted her lips with my tongue. I was like a chisel needing to be driven deep inside her. Placing my hand against the cold tile to steady myself, I wrapped my free arm around her waist and in one movement lifted her upward while keeping my lips on hers. Her legs wrapped tightly around my waist. Holding back as long as I could, I slipped my cock inside her. I heard her gasp at the sudden intrusion. It was then that I realized I didn't have a condom on. "Shit, baby, I'm sorry. Don't go away." I could have kicked myself in the ass for forgetting to sheath myself.

Just as I was ready to lower her to the shower floor, I heard her plead, "Don't go. I need to feel you, Lou."

Not even my willpower could stop me from taking her. I just needed to control my release and pull out before it was too late, Guiding my cock back inside her warmth. I took it slow and easy. I wanted to feel every inch of her warmth. Feeling her skin on skin with nothing between us was like paradise. I could feel the strength of her walls tightening, letting me know that she was close. "Hold on, baby," I commanded.

The minute I felt her body jerk, I knew she was met with her release as she clamped down, pulling me in further. As much as I wanted to continue feeling her, I knew my own release was close. Pulling from her body, I took my cock in my hand and finished what I couldn't do inside her. With her body so close to mine, my release spilled against her body, coating her wet skin with my seed.

~****~

It was almost noon and soon the taxi would be at the shop to take Emma to St. Andrew's. The tension in the shop was so thick, you could cut it with a knife. The floor would also soon need to be replaced with all the pacing that was going on. Hearing the honking of the taxi, I walked with Emma to the door. I could tell by the look on her face that she was scared. Pulling her close to me, I kissed her on the lips. "Everything will be fine, baby. Just follow the plan. The minute things don't feel right, remove your hat. We will be watching you the whole time," I assured her, looking over to Cop, Sly, and Peter.

Watching Emma get inside that taxi was the worst thing I had to go through. Even though I reassured her that everything would be okay, I knew there was that chance that something could happen to her. Finding out that Courtney wasn't at her apartment and seeing that there might have been some sort of struggle just made the stakes that something could go wrong even higher.

As the taxi drove away, we all got in our own vehicles and followed the taxi, keeping a safe distance behind it so as not to draw any attention. It was only a ten minute drive to the church, and Sly and Cop broke off in a different direction, assuring them that they would be arriving and in place before Emma got there. Peter and I stayed behind the taxi until Emma was let off at the church. The only one of us they knew personally was myself, so with an added hat and sunglasses to conceal my face, I could stay a reasonable distance from the church and still be able to see what was going on. Peter was going to be outside the church pretending to be a homeless person begging for food and shelter. Whoever would have thought he could actually pull of the disguise Lilly had put together for him?

As I sat in my truck, keeping an eye out for any movement, the minutes felt like hours. While I was trying to tame down my uneasiness, the door to the church opened and there as bright as day was O'Malley, and TJ trying to conceal the gun he had pressed in Emma's side from Peter, who was acting like he didn't care about what was happening. I knew how hard it was for me to not get out of the truck and get Emma, so it had to be just as hard for Peter, being right there and unable to do anything.

One thing that we didn't expect was another person in this equation. A black Cadillac resembling the one at the hotel pulled up to the curb. TJ opened the back passenger door and forced Emma inside while O'Malley took the front passenger seat. Watching them drive away, my heart sank, knowing how scared Emma must have been. When the Cadillac was a safe distance away, Peter left his position and got into his Camaro that was parked across the street. I, on the other hand, put the truck into drive and pulled away from the curb in route to follow the car. So far everything was going as planned. There was no indication that O'Malley knew that he was being followed.

As I pulled around the block at St. Peter's, Cop and Sly were already in place. If I didn't know their vehicles, I would have thought they were just two guys having a friendly conversation across the street on the sidewalk. Peter thought that it was better to be out in the open than hiding. O'Malley wouldn't think twice about two guys carrying on with a conversation like he would two guys sitting in their vehicles. I thought it was a great point.

Looking on, I watched TJ and Emma exit the car with O'Malley close behind. Peter advised us not to make a move until they were out of sight. With the driver still waiting in the car, he was nothing more than an obstacle that needed to be removed. Cop and Sly walked across the street, pointing at the church and pretending they were having a heated discussion. As they pretended to throw punches at each other, the guy in the car was getting nervous and soon exited his car. Cop and Sly were within a foot of the Cadillac and Cop was about to punch Sly, making it look like he was going to fall on the hood. In order to take the driver out, they needed him out of the car. As the guy tried to break up the fight, which was stupid on his part, Sly and Cop, in unison, planted fists to his face, causing him to be knocked out.

Cop grabbed the keys from the ignition while Sly dragged his body to the back of the car. Popping the trunk open, Cop hoisted the driver's limp body into the trunk and closed it. It was safe to say he wouldn't be a problem. With a signal from Sly, Peter and I headed towards the church. Based on the layout, we knew that O'Malley would be toward the front of the chapel, far away from the entrance doors.

As we headed in, we listened for chatter and kept an eye out for any movement. Unless Courtney was already in the church, she wasn't with O'Malley when they arrived or when they left St. Andrew's. Looking around, there was no one in sight. We began heading in separate directions, with Sly checking the narthex, while Cop and Chavez headed down the hallway to the church library and offices. Peter and I remained just outside the chapel doors. Slowly opening the door, O'Malley's surprised face came into view as he lifted his head from whatever he was holding in his hands. It could only be one thing, the plates. As we approached with our guns drawn, TJ stepped into view with a gun held to Emma's head.

With a look of terror, Emma's eyes met mine. "They've got Courtney."

Before, I could say anything. Sly opened the door and said, "Had. She is safe with Chavez."

Keeping my eyes on O'Malley and my gun aimed at him, I could see Cop coming up behind Tommy. It was only after he said, "Drop the gun," that I knew Emma was going to be okay.

Tommy lowered his gun and let go of Emma. Cop was able to pull the gun away from Tommy before Emma began to make her way towards me. It was as though my life flashed in front of me. Emma was suddenly pulled back by O'Malley. The cloth that I assumed held the plates wasn't holding the plates at all, but a gun. I knew one thing; this asshole wasn't leaving this church alive with Emma. Just as O'Malley backed up with Emma in his clutch, I looked straight at her and yelled, "Now!" Just as I had taught her, she elbowed him in the side and lowered her body in a crouching position. Kicking back with her right leg, she caught him in the shin. The gun flew out of his hand as he began to fall backwards. I could have killed him, but I knew a life in prison was going to remind him every day of just what he did.

After everything had settled and TJ and O'Malley were in the custody of the authorities, information about the plates surfaced. It was funny how karma worked. Turns out, there were never any plates at all. Seems the counterfeit money was made from 3D software and the instructions on how to make it and where to purchase the paper were on a thumb drive that was also in the cloth that O'Malley had pulled the gun from.

~****~

"Baby, we are just going to a welcome home party. Wear whatever you feel comfortable in," I stated as I watched Emma pull out every outfit she owned from the closet.

"Gainer, don't you dare start. This is important to me. I know how much these guys mean to you, and I want to make a good impression on Ash and his new wife Juliette," she said with a raised brow, which was sexy as hell.

Pulling her onto the bed, I swept away a stray piece of hair from her concerned face. "Baby, they are going to love you no matter what you wear. Besides, this will go with anything," I stated as I reached in my pocket and pulled out a solitaire diamond dressed with baguettes along the sides.

I wish I could have captured the look on her face. I think first she was confused, which soon turned into surprise, and then joy. In all my life, I had never met a woman with more emotions than this beautiful woman. As I scooted off of the bed so I could kneel before her, her eyes were still on the ring, but were now filled with tears. Taking her hand, I told her what she meant to me and how much she had changed my life. "Emma, my sweet Emma. The day that I practically ran you down in Central Park was the day you completely changed my life. Never had I met a woman with so much heart and compassion to fill the universe. You have freed me in so many ways. I couldn't imagine spending one day without you in my life. Emma Atwood, will you marry me?"

Placing the ring on her finger as best as I could, since it was shaking like a leaf, my eyes met hers. There were tears of joy spilling from her eyes. Placing her hand on her heart, she took her other hand and placed it on my cheek. "I would have married you the day we met. On that day, you saved me too."

Without a word, I picked her up and moved her closer to the head of the bed. Towering over her, I smiled and whispered, "I guess this means we are going to be a little late for the party," before claiming her as only mine.

About the Author

Some would call me a little naughty but I see myself as a writer of spicy thoughts. Being an erotic romance writer is something that I never imagined I would be doing. There is nothing more rewarding than to put your thoughts down and share them. I began writing four years ago and have enjoyed every minute of it. When I first began writing, I really wasn't sure what I was going to write. It didn't take me long to realize that romance would be my niche. I believe that every life deserves a little bit of romance, a little spice doesn't hurt either. When I am not writing, I enjoy the company of good friends and relaxing with a delicious glass of red wine.

I hope you found Gainer enjoyable to read. Please consider taking the time to share your thoughts and leave a review **http://amzn.to/2q3QLTS**. It would make the difference in helping another reader decide to read Gainer and all the books in the Jagged Edge Series.

To get up–to-date information on when the next Jagged Edge Series will be released click on the following link **http://allong6.wix.com/allongbooks** and add your information to my mailing list. There is also something extra for you when you join.

Gainer: Jagged Edge Series #6

Coming Soon!!!!!!

Chavez: Jagged Edge Series #7

Read all the books in the Jagged Edge Series

Hewitt: Jagged Edge Series #1
Cop: Jagged Edge Series #2
Hawk: Jagged Edge Series #3
Sly: Jagged Edge Series #4
Ash: Jagged Edge Series #5

Other books by A.L. Long

Shattered Innocence Trilogy

Next to Never: Shattered Innocence Trilogy
Next to Always: Shattered Innocence Trilogy, Book Two
Next to Forever: Shattered Innocence Trilogy, Book Three

To keep up with all the latest releases:

Twitter:

https://twitter.com/allong1963

Facebook:

http://www.facebook.com/ALLongbooks

Official Website:

http://www.allongbooks.com